MW00747803

Stage Business

A Novel by

Gerry Fostaty

Deux Voiliers Publishing
Aylmer, Quebec

This book is a work of fiction. Names, characters, businesses, organizations, places, events, and incidents are either the product of the author's imagination or are used fictitiously. Any resemblance to actual persons, living or dead, events, or locales is entirely coincidental.

First Edition Copyright © 2014 by Gerry Fostaty

All rights reserved.

Published in Canada by Deux Voiliers Publishing, Aylmer, Quebec.

www.deuxvoilierspublishing.com

Library and Archives Canada Cataloguing in Publication

Fostaty, Gerry, 1956-, author

Stage business : a novel / by Gerry Fostaty.

Issued in print and electronic formats.

ISBN 978-1-928049-08-1 (pbk.).--ISBN 978-1-928049-09-8

(Smashwoods)

I. Title.

PS8611.O7875S73 2014   C813'.6   C2014-906900-6

C2014-906901-4

Legal deposit – Bibliothèque et Archives nationales du Québec, 2014

Cover Design – Gerry Fostaty

Red Tuque Books distributes *Stage Business* in Canada. Please place your Canadian independent bookstore and library orders with RTB at www.redtuquebooks.ca

For Angie, of course.

Popularity is glory's small change.
Victor Hugo

Chapter 1

His parents were friends of a friend: a woman I was trying to impress. My friend's name was Amanda. She wasn't really a friend, but I was trying to change that. She worked with me. She was also an actor in the cast of the show I was rehearsing, so I couldn't impress her with my being an actor, with her being one, too. Besides that, she was much more successful than I was.

No one is ever really impressed by actors these days. Once you are beyond your twenties no one is awed by the choice of artistic poverty. People under thirty think that if you are not in Hollywood and famous, you are a failure, and people over thirty think that participating in art is a selfish affectation. Engaging in art, they think, is a hindrance to wealth and success, yet, at the same time, they believe owning art is a symbol of wealth and status. The pursuit of art itself holds no significance or importance anymore, only celebrity does. It doesn't matter if you are creating things or acts of beauty. What matters is how well known you are in the media. And, if you are cursed to be an artist in Canada, the one thing you can depend on is your anonymity. For most people who know me, my being an actor gives me an excellent excuse for my tired-looking clothing and my persistent neglect to pick up the cheque at dinner.

Amanda Clarke had never spoken to me before, other than to say hello at rehearsal. I was looking for any excuse to talk to her. She already had a solid career in the theatre, had done some movies, and was the voice of lots of radio and TV commercials.

She was beautiful, graceful, and a talented actor. She walked as if she had purpose, with long strides, and often stood with her feet planted apart while she listened to the scene being played on stage, or while receiving stage directions. On stage, she became the character, removing any trace of her real self and creating a persona that was entirely different, believable and immersive. Her irresistible, smoky voice reminded me of the taste of the burnt sugar on top of a Hungarian dobos cake. She was completely unaware of me, and of course, my interest in her.

So naturally, during a break at rehearsal, when she began telling the story of her friend's son gone missing, I hung on every word. I should have been studying my script on the break, instead of studying her ass from across the rehearsal room. I was spellbound by her shapely rear end as she wriggled out of her filmy, knee-length rehearsal skirt. As she carefully stepped out of it, wearing only black tights, leotard, and high-heeled character shoes, she looked like some Fosse-esque superhero. She bent over to pick up the skirt, and I swear she must have heard my jaw hit the floor, because she suddenly turned toward me. As soon as her head moved, I shot my eyes down to my script pages and tried to look like I was reading. I even moved my lips to make it more convincing.

"Michael, I'm sorry about walking all over your line, again," she smiled as she strolled over, holding the skirt and folding it lengthwise. "I was just trying to keep from dropping the pace in the scene."

"Oh, that's fine," I replied. She stood close enough for me to fully appreciate how penetrating her steel-grey eyes were. What she had

2

said about the scene suddenly struck me. "Oh, was I bogging things down?" God! The last thing I wanted was for her to think I was a burden. Even though we were in different scenes, one of the scene transitions was that the end of my line was picked up by her character on the other side of the stage as the beginning of her line.

"No, no, it was my fault. I'm just a bit distracted, today," she continued. "My friend's son has gone missing and I was up with her most of last night trying to calm her down. I haven't had much sleep and I can't help but think the worst." She dropped the skirt over the back of a nearby chair in exchange for her jeans while kicking off her shoes. "He didn't come home from school yesterday. They waited awhile, but by suppertime he still hadn't shown up and they started to call his friends' parents to see if he had stopped in."

"That must be frightening for them. No luck with the phone calls, I guess."

"None," she said. "No one has seen him. In fact, he wasn't even seen at school yesterday."

"Wait. Wouldn't the school have called home to report his absence?"

"That's what I asked," she said, looking at me as if I had read her mind, while she put a leg into the jeans. "They're supposed to call if you miss any of your classes, but yesterday there was no call."

"Any of your classes? He's in high school?" I asked while she sheathed another leg. "How old is he?"

"Seventeen."

The whole situation changed from being an Amber Alert to a joyride to the mall for a video game. At seventeen he was probably trying to score tickets for a concert, buy dope or booze, or there was a girl involved. If he was anything like the guys I grew up with, it was most likely all three.

She was slipping on the jeans now in a way that was devastating me: she slowly pulled the waistband up and over the curves of her hips while standing on her toes, then pulled the button toward the buttonhole. It was then that I made my mistake. In my clumsy attempt be charming I offered, "Is there anything I can do to help?" It was the button and her fly that I was getting at, but she mistook my suggestive remark for chivalry.

"I . . . I don't know," she faltered, and then smiled. "I'll let you know though. I'll have to see how things went today, you know, if they found him."

I hadn't seen this coming. This was better than I could have dared to imagine. I had stopped her in her tracks; she wasn't expecting that. Neither was I. Now I had a reason to talk to her, or rather, get her to talk to me. I could ask for updates on this kid.

"Five minutes!" yelled the stage manager from the prompt table at the foot of the stage. "Michael!" she called, indicating me with her chin. I gave her the high sign to let her know I would be right with her. When I turned back to Amanda, she was already hurrying away to get back to work. Oh well, I would slip in an offer to buy her coffee or lunch next time.

Our stage manager, Elizabeth Stackhouse, insisted we call her Bid. I have worked with a lot of stage managers in my career, and I have never worked with one that wasn't organized and capable. Bid, however, was clearly the best. She had a seriousness, talent and expertise that far exceeded her twenty-six years. She could get anything done and there was no demand that stumped her. She lived by the creed that she would make the easy stuff look hard, the hard stuff look easy, and a request for the impossible would always receive the response, "I'll make a call."

4

Bid was striding towards me, her arms full of script, notes, and rolls of coloured tape. Her Buddy Holly glasses teetered on the edge of her small freckled nose, making her tilt her head back to see me clearly as she approached. She wore her short cropped brown hair slightly scrunched with the merest hint of gel — her fashion statement. Her compact frame stopped abruptly in front of me, as she pushed her glasses up with her forearm and then poured her prompt book into my arms, taking me by surprise.

The stage manager's prompt book is a script filled with all the notes pertaining to the play. Besides all the lines in the play, there are things like costume notes, blocking (the movement and position of every actor and prop on stage), lighting and sound cues, timing, and of course, drawings of the set. In fact, the prompt book is the blueprint of the show. The prompt book never leaves the stage manager's sight unless it is locked in the theatre safe. As soon as she unloaded the book, she dropped onto her knees with a thud. She looked straight up at me and said, "Are you gonna move, or what?"

"Doesn't that hurt when you hit the ground like that?" I asked, wincing.

"Step back," she commanded, ignoring my remark and fanning me away with a limp hand movement. Her Buddy Hollys had made their way back to the tip of her nose again.

I ceremoniously took a step backward. She began tearing up some old shredded masking tape marks from the floor, sticking them to her sweatshirt, and replacing the beige marks on the floor with thin blue gaffer tape to indicate the position of a table. She stood to face me again, only a few centimetres away from me. She rolled the old tape into ball, then tossed it at her chair at the edge of the stage, hitting it square on the back, where it hung for a second before dropping to the seat.

5

"Two points," she said. Then, turning back to me, "You on or off for the next scene?" she abruptly asked while pushing up her glasses again and reclaiming the prompt book.

"On or off what?"

"Book. Are you on or off *book*?" She wanted to know if I had my lines memorized for the next scene.

"On." I gave her my best apologetic grimace.

"He's not going to like it," she cautioned, meaning the director. Before she turned away, she issued her warning. "He's given me a deadline to make sure you are all empty-handed by the end of next week. Don't make me look bad."

"Impossible," I said to her back as she strode away.

"Hmmm," was her final word.

The rest of the cast began to wander in to the rehearsal hall, and the chatter increased as the room filled. The play wasn't a large production and the cast wasn't huge; there were fifteen of us, but it was bigger than most shows running in Toronto at the time, excluding the big musicals like Wicked, or Phantom of the Opera. Amanda Clarke was among the few main characters. I was playing a supporting comic character, my specialty.

Amanda came back into the hall with the director, David Pound. Pound was tall and surely weighed over one hundred and fifty kilos. His imposing build was made even grander by his flamboyant gestures. Pound spoke to Amanda, leaning toward her as they walked, waving his hands while scowling and waited for her to respond. Amanda looked at him and nodded slowly in affirmation. She pulled out her small black notebook and began to scribble. Pound was off to give another note to someone else, bouncing off his heels in an attempt to make himself look lighter. It was the kind of walk that might prompt my mother to say that although he was heavy, he carried it well.

David Pound was pleasant and agreeable but was more of a good traffic cop on stage than a good director, keeping the look balanced and natural while preventing the actors from banging into each other and the furniture.

His formidable reputation was due to his genius at casting. Not only did he pick individual actors who would be right for the parts, he picked ensembles that would work so well together they would elevate his plays to greatness. Consequently, he used the same people again and again, giving the actors and the audience a sense of a repertory company. It meant that the cast worked very well together and quickly, and the audiences liked to come back to see these familiar faces in different shows and different roles. David Pound's shows never fought for an audience; in fact, most shows sold out. I felt very lucky for the steady employment his company offered.

He reached his desk at the front edge of the stage area and gestured to Bid with his hand before he sat down.

"Ladies and gentlemen!" Bid called out while standing in front of her chair. "Places, please, for Act Two!"

Nigel Holmes, another supporting cast member, drifted over to me at our spot on stage and handed me my script with a knowing look. He had been outside for a cigarette. The smell of stale smoke followed him.

"Was Bid giving you the gears?" he asked, raising an eyebrow.

"Yeah, I'm still on her list of malingerers."

"Don't fret. It's a large club. She is hitting us one by one, trying to make us feel as if we are the only ones still on book, playing on our guilt" he whispered while indicating the script in his hand.

"Very clever," I muttered. "How do you know this?"

"Ve have vays of finding out," he answered in a mock German accent. "Do you want to meet later and work the script over a few pints?"

"It's a deal," I said.

Bid sat at the stage management table, directly front and centre, pointed to Nigel, who had the first line in the scene, and cued him to begin. "Aaand, lights!"

Chapter 2

After rehearsal, I went straight home to do a little research on this kid, Kyle, who had gone missing. Amanda had given me his full name and approximate address when I offered to try to help out. Even if I couldn't find anything, I had the excuse I needed to speak to her again, giving me an opportunity to invite her out for coffee or lunch. Clearly, I was not above resorting to my high school tactics.

At home I popped open my laptop, ignoring the emails that streamed onto the screen. A calendar reminder popped open, blinking urgently: GET OFF BOOK!

"Later!" I said aloud to the computer. The cat took the sound of my voice as her cue to come into the room and begin howling at me. I figured I would distract her with some food while the Internet browser booted. I am pretty handy with my computer, researching the shows I audition for, the directors and their preferences, and the casting directors and their vices. Something I learned quite early as an actor is that talent is no guarantee of work. Getting noticed and having top-of-mind recognition with the casting agents are most important. The perpetually happy casting agents are a lost cause, but the grouchy ones are worth the bribes. About a week after they have said no is a good time to show up for some obscure reason, *I was just passing by and thought you might know someone who would like this . . . bottle of Scotch, box of smoked salmon, package of Belgian truffles.* The most effective bribes were hockey tickets. I found through careful research that a particular casting agent was a rabid Maple Leafs fan. I ended up in a CBC miniseries for those.

So, I figured researching a seventeen-year-old wouldn't be a problem. I knew the kid's name, I knew he was in high school, and I had an idea where he lived. I soon discovered the beauty of kids of his generation, Generation Y, is they crave celebrity status. A steady diet of pop idol gossip, YouTube videos, and reality TV has led them to believe that well-documented stupidity is a lifestyle and a path to success. They all seem to carry cameras to capture their questionable behaviour. The result is a trail on the Internet, making it easy to track them down. I wasn't long finding a few pages with Kyle's name, his picture, and some of his friends. There were hundreds of pictures. I followed a link to an old MySpace page where I found an address. He and many others made numerous references to meeting up on Palmerston on Friday nights. Bingo! I found the lead I needed. I grabbed my keys and set out to begin my sleuthing on Amanda's behalf.

She was looking at me as if I were the crazy one. Sure, I was staring at her. She looked to be about twenty, was pasty-skinned, and glowered back at me through eyes like slits. She stood in the doorway of her rundown Toronto apartment and she was almost naked. Well, she wore fingerless fishnet gloves and a pink thong, but the most striking features were the strategically placed tattoos and piercings. The tattoos covered most of her left side like a skin-tight bodysuit and the texture of the drawing made it look like armour. The ink began at her shoulder in a Celtic knot and graduated down her arm and chest, morphing from armour to scales, then into a dragon. A metal piercing was the only chink in the armour-like texture of the unlikely mix of styles and talent. Her lower torso featured leaves and flowers, and her left thigh sported a blonde forties-style pin-up, which began at her hip and ended near her knee. The whole package looked like a needlepoint sampler.

She stood, framed in the doorway, without a stitch of self-consciousness, her head jutting forward and wagging, her red painted lips slightly parted. Her eyebrows arched high over her squinting eyes in that universal expression that states, *I'm busy; you're bothering me.*

I noticed the head of the dragon was drawn so the eyes focused on the girl's face, its head rested on her breast, and its nose ended at her nipple. The startling piercing through her nipple made the dragon appear to have a ring in its nose. Too preoccupied with my own thoughts, I failed to respond to her bothered expression. She wagged her head more emphatically to get my attention.

"What?" she spat at me. I must have hesitated momentarily, and took a breath while trying to rationalize what I saw. As I set my lips to begin speaking, she reached up into her hair with both hands to undo a large hair clip. She was not overly concerned with me, other than I had interrupted her, despite her state of undress. Without taking her eyes off me she shook her head aggressively to loosen the mass of brown tangles held aloft with what I supposed was remnant hairspray. She took hold of the dishevelled hair, rewound it up like a rope, and replaced the clip. Her hair now fell in a ridiculous fantail. She had minimal makeup, just mascara and the bright red lipstick and she was pleasant looking, although I wouldn't have given her a second look except for the fact that she was unclothed. She finished her hair arrangement and did an abbreviated neck roll, her eyes never leaving mine.

"I'm Michael Dion. I'm looking for Kyle," I said trying to keep my eyes on her face, but she put her hand on her jutting hip to make a point of not looking uncomfortable. I responded by staying focussed on her heavy-lidded eyes, and attempting to look unaffected by her pushing the boundaries of modesty. This was clearly a new frontier for me. Thank God she broke the tension by speaking.

"Kyle isn't here," she said as she casually popped a knee forward over a perfect pedicure. Her elbow clumsily bumped the door and the door slowly swung wider, revealing her living room behind her. An eighteen- or twenty-year-old with a small camera around his neck was draping the walls and the furniture in the apartment with white sheets. He had the beginnings of a beard, all downy and sparse. With the beard and unkempt hair, as well as the tight black jeans and canvas running shoes, he wouldn't have looked out of place in a coffee house, circa 1965. He was standing on an aluminum ladder as the open door revealed him, reaching high up and clumsily pinning the sheet up on the wall with push-pins. He then began to drape the furniture. As he threw his arms out to cover the furniture, the camera around his neck would swing out on the lanyard and then swing back again, slamming into his collar bone or breastbone, making him wince each time.

"Getting ready to paint?" I asked indicating the inside of the apartment.

"It's a photo shoot," she offered in a condescending tone. "For Suicide Girls

"Suicide Girls?" This didn't sound good.

"It's a pin-up website," she elaborated.

"Ah, pin-up," I said pointing to the tat on her thigh. The unmistakable aroma of weed began to drift from the apartment.

"Kyle's not here," she said again, reaching to close the door.

"You're a model," I said, as though stating a fact. I tried to look impressed to keep her talking. The key to getting someone to open up is just get them talking about themselves. She tilted her head to the right, with her chin jutting out and stepped closer into the doorway.

"Yeah, I am . . . Well, I will be, once I get accepted on the site. Right now, I'm a hopeful. They have to vote me on."

"Who does?"

"The people who visit the website, the members. If they like my shots, they vote me on as a regular."

"I see. This pays well?"

"No, it doesn't pay at all, but we are allowed to accept gifts."

"Ah. Right," I said, not really understanding at all. "Have you seen Kyle today?"

"You a cop?

"No, just a friend."

"You don't look like a cop. Well, you look too much like a cop to be a cop. And your shoes are all wrong." She narrowed her eyes further, and slowed her speech with, "You don't look like a friend either." Then she closed one eye. "He owe you money?"

"Nope, I'm just trying to find him. Make sure he's all right. He's been away from home and his folks are worried."

"Why aren't they looking for him?" she snarled.

"They are," I said. "I'm just helping out." There was something about her that struck me as odd. My gaze was drawn momentarily to the camera guy. His sudden stillness tugged my focus. He finished his decorating, now stood in the living room, patiently waiting for her. He didn't step forward to offer help or even moral support. He just looked at her. It was as if he were her employee. I followed his gaze and had another look at her. Other than the tattoos and piercings, she struck me as quite mainstream. Her hair was uncoloured, and if it was allowed to hang down, would be unremarkable. She had a minimum of piercings on her face and even most of her tattoos would be covered if she was fully clothed. I quickly surveyed her extremities: hair, face, hands and feet — all unmarked, and it looked like she had recently had a manicure and pedicure.

"I haven't seen him since last weekend," she said, "I'm only really here on the weekends," which sounded odd.

"You know where he might be?"

"Nope."

"Do you think he might show up here soon?"

"Dunno . . ." She wasn't going to say any more. She sighed and rolled her eyes. Clearly, I was an inconvenience to her.

"Okay, thanks for your help. If he does come by, can you let him know his parents want to hear from him?"

"Yeah, yeah," she said while shaking her head. She started to grab for the door.

"You should get inside," I said indicating the rising nose on her dragon tattoo. "Looks like you're getting a chill."

After she slammed the thin door, I could hear her on the other side. "Fucking perv."

She would be no help at all, and probably wouldn't pass on the message.

I stood outside the Dragon Lady's apartment building on Palmerston Avenue. It was a four-storey walk-up, built in the nineteen-forties. With its dark red brick veneer and wooden sash windows it was probably a nice building back then. It still had some of the elegant wood trim and old doors, although most of its film-noire charm was hidden under too many coats of badly applied paint and cracking linoleum along the hallways. I was no further ahead

14

with my search than when I started. I still didn't know anything, but I had to give it up for now. There was a rehearsal at nine the next morning. I needed to be fresh, and I needed to go over my script. I was going to be on-book while the other actors in the cast would already be working their lines from memory. I had created this embarrassing problem myself by agreeing to help look for Kyle.

I glanced at my phone to see the time. It was time to meet Nigel to work on our scripts and drink some beer.

Chapter 3

I walked directly from the girl's apartment on Palmerston about seven blocks to the Boulevard Cafe on Harbord Street, and found a seat on the empty patio to wait for Nigel. I ordered a beer once the server finally noticed me and began to wade through my script. I knew Nigel would want to sit on the patio outside so he could smoke, and the absence of patrons made it the ideal place to rehearse our lines. I am one of those who have to read my script aloud to remember the lines. A teacher friend of mine says it's because I am an auditory learner. So, I either study aloud at home, or with a friend, or in a place where no one cares if you are talking to yourself. The Queen Street streetcar is a good place. Half of the passengers are already talking to themselves, and the other half are either on their cellphones or just don't care. If I am feeling especially self-conscious, I will study with my phone up to my ear.

I don't like to study at home because I never seem to get it done. My apartment is small and I am too easily distracted by things that I don't find distracting when I am not studying: like the dishes, the garbage, fixing something that is broken, or the cat. I don't mean fixing the cat, although that was certainly on the agenda in the near future. Even though I have a cat, I am definitely not a cat person. The cat arrived with a roommate I once had. She was also an actor, and getting ready to go on a cross-country tour, so she only needed a place to live for a short time. She showed up on moving day with a kitten. We weren't involved in any romantic way; we just shared an apartment for a while. I was recently divorced and needed a roommate. I was used to living with someone, needed help with the rent, and she needed a place to live, having just come out of her own domestic drama. Before she went on the road, she asked me to take care of her little fiend until she got back. I admit, she used the word *friend*. I was in a long-running show that was not scheduled to go on tour, so I knew I wouldn't be leaving town until at least after she got back. Naturally, I said yes. She never came back, and the cat is still with me. A friend tells me the cat is a long-haired tabby. She wasn't named before the woman who owns her left, and I never felt I had the right to usurp her owner's responsibility. Really, I have no need to name her. I never call her; I don't have to. She is always around. She is small but full of character; that is to say, she likes to climb the curtains and claw at the furniture. She has ruined my couch already, and is working on the armchair. I used to chase the cat away from the furniture with a spray bottle, but she began waiting until I was out of the apartment. Consequently, the cat and I don't get along. From the way the cat treats me I can tell she blames me for the breakdown in our relationship. We have come to accept that we both live alone, just under the same roof.

I would have phoned Nigel to see what was keeping him, but my decrepit phone was charging at an outlet under the next table. The server came back to ask if I wanted another beer just as Nigel waved from the sidewalk. My glass wasn't yet half empty so I declined, but I ordered one for him as he made his way over to the table.

Nigel and I are both in our early thirties, but he never tires of telling anyone who will listen that he is much younger than me. He insists that I was born old. Tall and slim, his dark eyes are penetrating and can suggest intensity and a dangerous personality, but can change in a flicker to playful mischief. Most days, his dark hair, cut short on the sides though longish on the top, looks like it has never seen a brush.

He came to Canada from England with his parents when he was a young boy. He conveniently retains just a hint of an English accent and uses it mostly when he wants to be condescending, or when he plays an English character on stage. He says he hates being typecast as an Englishman, but like any actor, he is thankful for any job, so he never protests very loudly. He is a great character actor and changes entirely from show to show. He is also a master of his makeup box, completely remaking himself in each character, inside and out. He is extremely fit, too, enjoys high adventure activities like skydiving and bungee jumping, and runs marathons a few times a year, but he pretends that he is a couch potato and feigns laziness and sloth. He also smokes, which I find incongruous, given his fitness regime.

"What are we drinking?" he asked rubbing his hands together as the server clunked down the glass in front of him.

"Draft," I said as I stretched toward another table to get him a foil ashtray.

"Not Stella?" he said disappointedly, while sliding a cigarette out of the package.

"You buying?"

"Draft it is!" he proclaimed as he raised his glass in a toast.

Nigel and I cracked open our scripts to a scene we shared and began to work the lines, breaking only for me to order additional pints and he to light cigarettes. I liked to watch him read his lines while his teeth were clamped on a cigarette. It gives the reading a different, hardened sounding character. Also, he has to squint as the cigarette smoke stings his eyes. He always pretends he isn't bothered by it. He knows I will seize on any complaint and chastise him again for smoking. I didn't wait this time for him to complain; his eyes were watering as if he'd been attacked with tear gas.

"You'll have to quit those one day," I reminded him, "or you're going to end up with smoke-cured eyeballs." He waved me off with a flourish. It wasn't long before the ashtray filled and I had to go to another table for a replacement. The server pointedly ignored the ashtray.

"Look at these bloody things," said Nigel picking up the fresh ashtray and throwing it down on the table like a gauntlet. "Foil, for God's sake. Gone are the days of the elegant glass ashtray. We smokers are marginalized." He shook his head in disgust. "Next, they'll be serving us beer in bloody Styrofoam."

The evening was unusually warm for late September in Toronto, so we didn't notice the sun setting. As we worked our way through the pages of the play, we were too absorbed to realize the patio had filled with patrons. We tried to focus on the scenes that would be next in the rehearsal schedule, hoping to have those at least partially memorized by the next time we were on the rehearsal stage to avoid Bid's wrath.

A cellphone set to loud started ringing at the next table. The people at the table made no attempt to answer it or even mute the ringer. I turned to glare at them, but they were too busy looking under the table for the endlessly ringing phone. I quickly realized it was my phone, evidently fully charged now. The people at the next table weren't terribly pleased, either, as I groped and crawled about under their table to retrieve my phone and charger.

"Sorry about that," I offered weakly as I retreated back to our table. *Unknown number* the screen read. Just as I put it down, it rang again.

"It's Atom Egoyan," Nigel boomed so the whole patio could hear. "He's doing a film about Noah's Ark. He wants you to play both unicorns . . . "

"Hello?" I answered the phone.

"Michael? It's Amanda."

"They're twin unicorns," Nigel continued loudly, "both male, but one is in drag. They know about the impending flood and they're trying to convince Noah that . . ."

"Amanda . . . Hi . . ." I waved my hand to try and quiet him. "This is a surprise. I didn't know you had my number."

"I got it off the call sheet," she said. "Where are you?"

"I am at the Boulevard with Nigel. We're just going over the script and having a few —"

"Oh! I'm right around the corner. I'll be right there." She hung up.

"Amanda?" Nigel eyebrows neared his hairline. "Amanda Clarke? Hmmmm!" His voice oscillated as a taunt.

"Yes," I said, trying to sound annoyed, as I flipped my phone closed. "She sort of asked me for a favour and I was going to report back to her tomorrow at rehearsal. I guess she got impatient."

"Report back? Impatient? What are you two up to?" His left eyebrow arched again.

"It's not what you think. Actually, it's not what I think — I have no idea what is really going on." I was about to launch into the story when Amanda burst onto the patio cradling a loaf of rye bread like a football.

"You really were around the corner," I said to her.

20

"I was at the bakery. How can you both sit here? Aren't you cold?" she exclaimed. She was wearing a light suede jacket and a silky burgundy scarf. Her hair was tied back in a ponytail. She looked fantastic.

For the first time I realized it had grown cool and I noticed the world had darkened beyond the edge of the lighted patio.

"All right, let's find a spot inside," groaned Nigel as he stood. "But I can't smoke inside. The smoker will unselfishly be marginalized, once again, for the sake of your comfort." I'm sure he thought he sounded like a martyr.

A group just paying as we got inside would free up a semi-circular booth. We hovered by their table as they scooped up their things and buttoned up their jackets to leave. They hadn't taken three steps away before we tucked ourselves into the cozy booth, with Amanda between us. I began to apologize.

"I was going to let you know what happened when I saw you tomorrow morning at rehearsal. It wasn't much anyway, but I guess I should have given you an update right away," I said.

"No, I've been trying to get you on the phone all evening," she said, "but there was no answer."

"His phone has been ringing all evening, but he refuses to answer it," Nigel slurred just a bit. "It's that damned Egoyan. He wants Michael for the new film." He winked at me.

"Really?" she asked, looking impressed.

"No," I said dismissively. "Pay no attention to him. My phone battery was dead and I was charging it. I didn't have any luck tonight, though. I stopped by the apartment of one of Kyle's friends, and she hasn't seen him since last weekend. He does have one pretty strange friend, though."

"How did you know where to look for his friends?" she asked.

"I just got lucky while looking around on the Web," I said.

"Who is Kyle, and what about these strange friends?" asked Nigel, leaning forward and looking interested.

Amanda told him about her friend Karen and her friend's son, Kyle. Then she started to apologize to me. "I'm sorry to have had you running around like that, but they found him. He was asleep on a couch in their basement. Apparently, he was awake all night on some video gaming website tournament and then just slept through the whole day."

"That explains why the Dragon Lady hasn't seen him," I said.

"Who's the Dragon Lady?" asked Nigel.

I told them about my encounter with the tattooed girl.

"She sounds like a Trustafarian," mused Nigel. Our blank looks must have been telling, so he continued. "She is one of those weekend urchins, a suburban middle-class kid with a trust fund who dresses down and slums it on the weekends when the part-time poverty persona suits her — half trust fund, half bohemian — a Trustafarian."

Nigel thought this was great fun, of course, and wanted to know her address. "I'll go over and pretend I'm doing a survey," he said.

"Forget it," I said. "Well, at least your friend's son is safe. All's well that . . ."

"Don't." Nigel was holding up both hands. "Don't lower yourself."

Amanda laughed. "What are we drinking, I'm buying."

"Er . . . Stella," said Nigel in his plummiest tone.

Chapter 4

Actors will do anything if they think it will increase the chance of getting a part. Dressing for the part at an audition is one thing, but sometimes it can go well beyond that. A few months before this, I was sitting at an audition waiting for my turn to go in. I was completely unsuited for the job, but I think my agent sent me to the audition in the hopes that it would stop me from pestering her with phone calls for a while. We always have to be looking for the next show or the next job, and much of that burden of finding those opportunities falls on our agents.

My agent, Brandi Weiss, had only recently come over to the legitimate theatrical side from the seedier burlesque side. She was used to handling strippers and mistakenly thought actors had the same interchangeability that the peelers had. She looked like an agent character from an old black-and-white film with her unnaturally brown dyed hair, too much black eyeliner, and pinched smoker's mouth masked with red-brown lipstick. Underneath her hardened exterior, though, you could still glimpse a one-time great beauty, but those days were long gone. She perpetually held a cigarette in her mouth, whether lit or not, and wore her hair up in a tight bun that always had a pen stuck through it. Her few clients looked like the dregs of the artistic community; her office waiting room resembled the Island of Misfit Toys. She had a habit of throwing her clients at any audition in the hope something would stick. Though she often sent me for auditions for which I was completely unsuited, once in a while, she landed me a job. When I would question my suitability for a role, she would counter with, "You know you're not right for the part, and I know it, but maybe they don't know it." Then she'd shrug and hand me the audition script.

This time it was a beer commercial. The setting of this beer commercial was a bar where two competing soccer teams were enjoying a beer after their hard-played game. The premise was that whatever rivalry there was during the game, all was genial when they had a beer together afterwards.

As usual there were many of us auditioning for the commercial and we were asked to show up for the audition at an advertising agency, on the eighth floor of a Yonge Street office building, dressed for soccer. The waiting room was crowded, and most of us were wearing athletic shorts and knee socks with a tee shirt. The group of auditionees was roughly divided in half. One half were actors like me: youngish and somewhat fit. The others might have been actual soccer players. I don't know where they found these guys. They were rough, really aggressive looking, built like trolls and gave the impression that they were well acquainted with beer drinking. Their breath suggested, too, that they had done a bit of hands-on research before they got to the audition. They were familiar with one another, and spoke in an eastern European language. They kept laughing at us while sneering, in an attempt to intimidate us. It didn't stop there, though. They also had the habit of elbowing us actors out of the way and roughly shoving us to the rear of the pack whenever the casting assistant came out looking for whoever was next in line.

We had quietly decided amongst ourselves to let these soccer hooligans go ahead of us and then, once they were all gone, we would audition in a civilized manner. There was no use complaining; we couldn't get close enough to even talk to the casting assistant. Anytime we would move forward, we would just be roughly heaved rearward again. It wasn't worth risking a black eye or broken ribs. A black eye would have ensured that we would be unsuitable candidates for the commercial anyway, and would prevent us from auditioning for anything else until the swelling and bruising had gone down. There were already a few bruises and crushed toes that had been *accidentally* stepped on. Their strategy was working. So we kept ourselves out of their way and on the chairs against the wall.

One of the younger actors was, like me, watching the soccer players from the safety of the line of chairs against the wall in the waiting room. He was starting to appear decidedly unwell. His face had gone white and his jaw became slack while he sat there. He started sweating and breathing noisily, and he began to groan softly, as if he was in pain.

"Are you all right?" I asked him quietly.

"Shhh. Keep it down." he groaned, and then said bravely, "I'll be okay."

"What's the matter?" I asked him, trying to keep my voice down.

"I wanted to look youthful and fresh-faced for the audition," he said moaning softly, and then pulling his knees up to his chest, suddenly. "So I drank a litre of milk: you know, to give myself a rosy complexion, but this is taking longer than I calculated." He moaned again. "I usually have about an hour."

"What do you mean you usually have about an hour?" I asked a little alarmed. Whoever heard that drinking a litre of milk would make you look rosy?

25

"I'm lactose intolerant," he winced. "My stomach can't tolerate milk. I've been here too long and my stomach is starting to rebel, but I can't leave; I don't want to lose my place in line."

This was the most ridiculous thing I had ever heard, but I had no time to tell him that, even if I had wanted to. There was no time for me to react. In my wildest dreams I couldn't have anticipated what was about to happen. Thank God I was sitting beside him and out of the line of fire, because it all happened too fast. The casting assistant had just come into the room and the soccer players had once again just rushed ahead of us to ensure that we had no chance with her. It was as if a dam had burst. The fact that he was wearing soccer shorts and his knees were at his chest, meant there was no impediment to the flow that issued from beneath him. The hem of his shorts must have acted like a ski jump and directed the flow up and squarely at the backs of the clutch of the soccer hooligans. He must have surprised himself, too, because he leapt to his feet, shrieking in horror. One of the hooligans turned to face him. The hooligan's face was twisted with disbelief, then shock and rage, and he looked like he was about to throttle the young actor. He took a step toward us but slipped in the foul, warm puddle and went down. He screamed in a fury. The smell was overpowering. Everyone stood there stunned, trying to think of some way to salvage this situation. There was no need. It was about to get worse. The other end of him then erupted like a hydrant and he began running as he vomited. The crowd parted in front of him as he ran, scooping up his resume and photo off the casting assistant's table, presumably so he wouldn't be identifiable once it was all over.

The day was a dead loss. Everyone was sent home. I don't know if they ever even shot that commercial. I never saw it. I don't know how that poor actor got home in that state and I never saw him at an audition again. I also vowed never to drink milk before an audition.

The rehearsal hall for the show we were preparing was located in a church basement in the east end of Toronto, just a short walk from the Queen and Broadview streetcar stop. The old church was well situated, surrounded by the requisite restaurants and coffee shops. The numerous large basement rooms were regularly rented out to theatre companies. The high ceiling handily accommodated larger sets, or scenes that involved any sort of acrobatics, dancing, or fighting with weapons. It was a good arrangement for theatre companies because rent was cheap and the rooms could house large shows. Rehearsal space in theatres was very expensive and usually unavailable because of currently running productions. Churches benefited, too, because the arrangement provided them with a steady source of income.

This week, our church basement was full. Besides our show, there was a children's theatre company preparing for a country-wide tour, a company auditioning for a musical, and an industrial show rehearsing for an upcoming plumbing fixtures trade show. The children's company was rehearsing a puppet show with large, full-sized Muppet-like characters. The actor-puppeteers, always dressed in black, wore knee pads and black balaclavas.

The auditions had a smaller room with a long line of chairs outside the door and down the hall. The chairs were filled with tense and frightened-looking actors who mumbled lines from their audition pieces to themselves, or paced up and down the hall while trying in vain to hide the terror on their faces. Most of them looked like they had raided their local Goodwill store the day before, to come up with what they thought might be suitable for their audition.

Nigel and I met at the front door to the church on the way into rehearsal. On our way down the hall, one of the guys auditioning for the musical pulled me aside to quietly ask if he could borrow my leather jacket for the audition.

Although we weren't friends, I knew who he was and had seen him around. The acting community in Toronto isn't small, but we all seem to regularly make the same rounds. I hoped someone would do the same for me if I needed a similar favour.

"Your leather jacket will be perfect for the character," he beamed.

I slipped off my jacket while asking him what he was auditioning for.

"The dentist," he replied shakily.

Occasionally, if the action was heated or if there was a big musical number, the sounds of one rehearsing group would bleed into another room. At those times, rehearsal became an exercise in focus and concentration, especially when the industrial show folks began to sing about the lower litres-per-flush of the toilets and the eco-friendly waterless urinals, as they were when Nigel and I passed their open door.

The puppeteers, walking in the opposite direction and holding their puppets high over their shoulders in working position, greeted us in the hallway. The puppets, made of foam, fur, and feathers, were remarkably detailed and striking close up, and we stopped to admire them and talk for a few minutes. Thankfully, they didn't stoop to speaking to us through the puppets; although, the puppets' eyes focused back and forth on whichever one of us was speaking, sometimes nodding gently in agreement. One of the puppets looked at its watch, which prompted the puppeteer to say it was time to get back. They continued down the hall away from us, with the puppets bouncing just enough to leave us with the impression they were walking. The black-clad puppeteers glided after them like their ninja servants.

Chapter 5

"Good morning, Bid," bellowed Nigel as we entered our rehearsal hall. Bid was always in first in the morning. No matter how early I arrived, she was always there before me, writing in the prompt book, setting props, or moving tables around. I liked to arrive for work early, and I always found her looking busy.

"What are you doing here?" she was looking at her watch. "You're not called until eleven."

"We're keeners, apple polishers, brown n . . ." chirped Nigel.

"We came in to work the script," I interrupted before he went on. "We're attempting to get off book before we embarrass you."

"Don't tease me," Bid replied. I started walking toward the back of the hall to find a place out of the way to work when she called out, "Are you joining the musicians' union? You sound like a percussionist. What's in your pockets, man, maracas?"

"I . . . what?" I slapped my pockets. A package of Tic Tacs in my right pocket was the rattling culprit. I pulled the nearly empty container out and faced her. "Mint?" I offered her one.

"Thanks." She held her hand out to accept the mint. "Now get rid of them. I don't want you sounding like a rogue rhythm section during my rehearsal."

I considered putting them on a table but I knew they would either disappear or I would just forget them, so I shook what was left into my pocket. Then I tossed the plastic package into the garbage can beside her table. "Two points!" I declared.

"One point," said Bid shaking her head. "You were inside the line."

By the end of the day a transformation in the show had taken place. The church basement chairs and tables we had been using initially had been replaced by the actual stage pieces. There were larger set pieces like walls and staircases that the crew had lugged in overnight, so we could work on timing and sightlines. The cast was starting to wear bits and pieces of our costumes: shoes, hats, and character defining parts of our apparel. The cast, too, was coming together. Most of the actors were now off book; Nigel and I were almost there.

Tamara, the wardrobe assistant, trundled across the room laden with a stack of costume pieces. She was craning her neck to try to keep her chin on top of the pile, steadying it, as she made her way toward me. She stopped and the pile toppled on the table beside me. Once her hands were free, she pulled a tape measure from her back pocket and flipped it over her head to let it drape around her neck. She was wearing what looked like a fishing vest, the pockets bulging with spools of thread, a roll of elastic waistband, and cards of buttons. The vest front was covered in a variety of pins and needles preloaded with different colours of thread carefully wound in skeins behind each one. She reached into the pile and fished out a pair of pants for me.

"There's a name tag with your name on it, on the waistband," she said flatly as she handed me the pants. "Don't remove it. Just try them on and leave them on, unless they're too tight to get on. If they're too big, leave them on until I get a chance to get back to have a look. Got it?" Then she was off, even before I could nod my assent.

The actual rehearsal part of the day was over. Once the costumes arrive for their first appearance, there is too much of a distraction to do anything else and it is best to get all the objections, obstacles, and laughs out of the way at the same time.

Amanda stood at the other side of the hall dressed in her full costume. The long rehearsal skirt that she wore earlier had been replaced by a forties' style business suit, a grey tweed skirt and a short jacket, topped with a pillbox hat. She was talking to Tamara who arranged the hat's tulle netting in the front to rest just below Amanda's eye line. Then she passed the hat to Tamara who carefully placed it in a box. Tamara waved her finger in my direction before making a note on her pad and heading off with her pile to someone else. Amanda gathered up her clothes and headed toward me. We hadn't spoken for a few days, other than to exchange hellos or waves from across a room. I just could not find an opportunity to start a conversation without sounding like I was angling for an opportunity to start a conversation. She stopped on the other side of the table beside me, where she slipped her jeans on under her costume and then flipped off the skirt to drop it on the table.

"This is the repair pile," she said. "It needs to be taken in at the waist. Looks like yours do, too." I was holding up the baggy pants, waiting for Tamara to make her way back to me. They were a bit big, but my character called for a more dishevelled and rustic look.

"I'm thinking of wearing a ball cap backwards with these pants," I said trying to sound playful. "I'm going for a more contemporary, urban gangster look."

"Ah, you mean 'gangsta'," she countered.

"Didn't I say that?"

31

"Almost."

"How are your friend and her sleepy son?" I ventured, trying to maximize my time with her and maybe slip in a lunch invitation before she could escape.

"Fine, I guess," she sighed. "I haven't heard anything from Karen over the past little while, but with Kyle, there's always something. At least she knows where he is lately — well, most of the time, anyway. He's been giving them grief over the last few years, issues with school, drugs, and he thinks nothing of stealing their money or grabbing the car keys in the middle of the night when they're asleep to go for a ride. It wouldn't be so bad if he had his driver's licence. They are going to try to reconnect this weekend, apparently, at a secluded cabin they rented for the summer. They're going to try to be together without any distractions — not even any cellphone service — to see if they can re-bond." Amanda made air quotes and then shrugged her shoulders.

"That's a tall order for a short weekend," I said.

"It's all they have. They both have to work on Monday."

"How long have you known them?" I asked.

"Oh, Karen and I went to high school together," she said. "We've taken different paths in life, but we've stayed in contact. She's my oldest friend."

I was about to take the plunge and offer lunch or dinner, but Tamara was back and took me by surprise. She didn't say a word. She just stepped in between Amanda and me, firmly grabbed my waistband on either side and after a vigorous shake, began pinning the pants. She took a step back and looked me straight in the pelvis. "You're hanging a bit low in the crotch," she said with a pin in her mouth.

"Thanks," I replied.

32

"Oh, get over yourself. I need to measure your crotch depth. Sit on this chair," she barked. She had heard it all before.

I had no idea what she was up to, but she was a woman in a hurry and not to be messed with. I had heard stories from actors who pissed off the wardrobe people and then were surprised, usually during a scene, by strategically placed pins in their costumes that would reveal themselves as if they had a time delay fuse. There is nothing more startling, I had heard from the injured, than being suddenly surprised by a pin in the arse or crotch. I sat down as I was told. She grabbed a flat metal bracelet from her wrist that straightened with a snap into a ruler. She laid the ruler against my hip as I sat there, measuring from the top of the waistband to the chair. She then slapped the ruler against her wrist and it immediately curled back into a bracelet. "Leave the pants on this table," she instructed. She scribbled a note in her pad and was gone.

"Ladies and gentlemen!" Bid crowed from the middle of the room. "Thank you all very much for your hard work this week. We will see each other Monday at nine a.m. Have a great weekend." She shot me a look from her spot while she wrote down something on her clipboard. "Michael! Michael Dion!" she said holding up her index finger. I nodded back. She wanted to see me about something.

"See you on Monday," Amanda smiled at me, while she scooped up her things and flew toward the exit. I'd missed my chance, again. I was out of luck until next week.

Once I had dropped my costume pants back onto the repair pile, I worked my way over to Bid and waited as the crowd around her thinned. She was surrounded by a few people, while making notes and giving some final instructions to some crew members. She was organizing more set pieces to be brought in over the weekend. Once she had dealt with everyone else, she turned to me.

"Thanks for your work on the script this week," she said quietly and then began writing. "I appreciate the fact that you're off book." She continued scribbling.

"I had to get there sooner or later," I said. "It might as well be sooner."

"Right," she said, as she snapped her notebook closed. She looked me straight in the eyes and said, "Well, have a good weekend." Then quickly, she continued. "You're not going to regress on me come Monday, are you? You'll still be empty-handed, I hope."

"I'm going to continue to work on it all weekend, I promise."

"Okay, see you." She shooed me out so she could lock up.

A bit odd, but stage managers are a bit odd. Neither cast nor crew, they dwell in the middle, alone.

Like Bid, I was solitary, too, at the moment. Actors live strange and ever-changing lives. Out of work they are inconsolable and miserable to live with. Working, they are busy and happy, though neurotic and miserable to live with. Those were some of the reasons my marriage broke down. My ex-wife is a terrific person, but she is not an actor, or involved in the arts. She works in the financial industry. Although she tried, she could never come to terms with the vulnerability and fragility of an actor's spirit and ego, and I made no serious attempt at bridging the gap between us. However stable and confident actors look on the exterior, there always looms a hidden frailty, ready to be exposed in private. Then, there are the crazy work hours, and the months of touring, the weeks away shooting films on location and, of course, the fact that they spend so much time trying to create a character for the role they are working on. In addition, they have to try to factor in a confident persona for the casting people, directors, and producers. My ex wasn't prepared for me to breeze in and out of town when my schedule allowed, only having to get reacquainted after so many months away. At the same time, I would have been trying to adjust to being at home again and sorting out the hierarchy of my split personalities. All that uncertainty was no way to start a family. That, of course, was the other thing. She wanted to start a family, and I thought that if I could just get my career sufficiently ramped up toward success, we would be in a better position to have children.

We parted well, or as well as you can when a marriage ends, and I still manage to talk to her once in a while, usually at events that involve mutual friends, like weddings and funerals, but it is getting less and less frequent as the years progress. She has a new man in her life. She hasn't told me much about him. I think she is uncomfortable speaking about him, and she doesn't want him to be uncomfortable about me. I had heard through a mutual friend that they were going to start a family. I am still trying to ramp up my career.

The climb to the mirage of artistic success, though, is never-ending.

Chapter 6

I planned to relax all weekend with my script, take it with me
wherever I went: the laundromat, the grocery store, restaurants. If I
went to a movie, I would read it before the trailers began and, of
course, en route on the bus and subway. I intended to take it easy, but
whenever I found myself idle, I would pull out my script and study to
solidify the work I had already done to get off book, so I could stay
off book.

When I am in rehearsal, the weekdays are hectic. Rehearsals take
the full day; there is travel time, and study time that always keeps me
moving and busy until I go to bed at night. I knew as we got closer to
the show's opening night, our workday would extend from eight to
twelve hours. The days are exhausting and you are happy to fall into
bed at night. Once the show started running, we would have to be at
the theatre when most people head home from work or at noon for the
matinees. And every night, we would work until close to midnight.
The days, once the current show is running, are taken up looking for
the next show, commercial or film, auditioning, and gently pestering
your agent. So the weekends, when I am in rehearsal, are a time to
enjoy and relax. I was going to take full advantage of this weekend. I

was going to get to bed at a reasonable hour and start on my script in earnest in the morning.

My good intentions, though, were foiled when my phone woke me up early Saturday morning. I had no idea what I was in for. If I had had any inkling, I would have smashed the phone with a large hammer and rolled over, instead of picking it up "Hello?" I was speaking even before the phone was at my ear.

"Michael? Is that you?"

"The last time I looked," I moaned. "Who is this?" I couldn't find the alarm clock to see what time it was. I started to reach around, groping under the bed, and ended up with a handful of cat. The cat, unimpressed by my invasion of her privacy, hissed and swatted me with her claws out, catching my wrist.

"It's Amanda. You sound different. Can I come over?"

"Sure," I said. "Now?"

"Right now." She sounded frazzled and serious.

"Okay, I live on . . ."

"I have your address. I'll be there soon." The phone went dead and my heart sped up.

What did *soon* mean? I didn't know how much time I had before she arrived, so I sprinted to the kitchen and put on a pot of coffee. Then I jumped into the shower and set a record for the shortest amount of time under running water. I threw some clothes on while running around the living room, kicking loose things under furniture. The cat supervised me from the back of the couch. I had time to set a couple of mugs and spoons on the table and was pulling my socks on when the door buzzer sounded.

I was still out of breath when she walked through the door and began pacing, apologizing for waking me up. I couldn't help but notice that even in her troubled state, she was beautiful. I didn't know what to do with myself while she paced, so I went to get the coffee pot.

"He's gone again," she said abruptly. "This time it is serious."

"Who is gone?"

"Kyle, the boy," she said. "My friend's son. And this time, it's my fault."

"You? Why?"

"I told Karen to stand up to him. She said he is always threatening to move out, so I told her to call his bluff. Well, she did, and now he's gone. Shit! What have I done? I don't have any kids. I have no right to give any advice on child rearing!" she said, throwing her hands up in defeat. "I certainly didn't expect anyone to take my advice. Shit! Shit! Shit!"

"Wait, start at the beginning." I said. "Let me pour some coffee and we'll take this from the top." I was still trying to clear my head from being jolted out of bed and having Amanda land on my doorstep. As I put a full coffee mug in front of her I said, "The last thing I heard you say about this was they were heading to a cabin to have a little quality time. That was yesterday. So what happened?"

"They went to the cabin, but of course Kyle went under protest," began Amanda, hotly. "He said he wanted to stay in town, that he had made plans to go out with friends. Karen said that was just what she wanted to keep him from, his friends. She told him he was going with them, and that was that. She is very assertive. Everyone says that about her. When she has her mind made up, there is no changing it, you know."

"So, she forced him into it," I said, trying to get to the point.

"Don't judge her." Amanda was pointing her finger at me. "She was thinking of her son's well-being." She paused and made a movement with her hands to indicate she was calming down. "They all went to the cabin."

"And?"

"Karen said the car was deadly quiet on the way up. They didn't even play any music in the car. Karen and her husband Rob thought the silence would spark conversation. All it meant, though, was that Kyle plugged himself into his iPod and ignored them for the three–hour drive to the marina. They have to take a boat to the island where the cabin is."

"Did they get there?"

"They did," she sighed. "They were unloading the luggage from the boat to their dock. Kyle was still sullen, refusing to help with the luggage and refusing to respond to Karen. He just put his earphones back in, turned up the volume, and turned his back on his mother. So, Karen snatched away the iPod to try to talk to him and that's when it blew up."

"She snatched it away?" I moved my hand in a swiping motion to clarify. Amanda nodded. I was starting to see how bad this was for Kyle. I remembered being seventeen and thinking my parents were a pair of drooling idiots. I could see that Kyle might feel Karen had backed him into a corner. "So, a fight broke out?" I asked, prompting her for more.

"Karen said she had never seen him so angry. He stormed around screaming, stomping, throwing things, kicking the luggage, and yelling obscenities at his parents. He tried to grab the iPod back from her. They tussled a bit, he ended up pushing his mother off balance, and she fell. She took that as an act of war and she hurled his iPod into the lake."

"What was Dad doing all this time?" I asked.

"Rob was just watching from the sidelines, I guess," said Amanda. "He has a tendency to let Karen act and then he reacts later, after she is out of steam."

"So, now the iPod is at the bottom of the lake," I reminded her. "The kid was naturally going to be pissed off. What then?"

"Karen said Kyle just calmed right down. He turned and walked away from the cabin. That's when she gave him the ultimatum either to turn around and face her or move out. He just kept going and headed into the woods. They figured they would let him calm down for a bit and then go and talk to him."

I was going to ask what happened when they finally spoke to him, but Amanda continued.

"Except they couldn't find him," she took a breath. "They waited a bit, as they had planned to, and then they went looking for him. They searched the area, and called out for him, but he didn't answer. At first, they thought he had gone deeper into the woods, so they followed the path in, but he must have been hiding and waiting for them to do that. He somehow doubled back, because while they were in the woods looking, they heard the boat engine start. They ran back to the dock just in time to see the boat take off at high speed across the lake. They assumed he was headed toward the marina about fifteen minutes away." She took a deeper breath. "That's the last time they saw him."

"Didn't they go after him? Ah wait, don't tell me. They only have one boat, right?" I said.

"No, there is another boat, but it's just a dinghy with a little motor." She said. "It took them well over an hour to get to the marina in that. Kyle was long gone. Luckily they hadn't left the keys in the car's ashtray as they usually do. Kyle would have taken the car and they would have been stranded up there."

"Did anyone see Kyle?" I asked. "At the marina, I mean."

"Yeah, the guy that runs the gas pump said he saw him heading for the road. They checked the road but they didn't see him. They figure he hitched a ride."

"You made it sound a bit remote up there," I said. "Do they think he might have hidden in the woods?"

"No, Karen told me he's not very fond of the outdoors," Amanda replied. "No, he would've wanted to get back to the city as soon as he could."

"So, let's say he hitchhiked back to town on a road that takes three hours to drive." I was trying to think this through logically. "It was still light out when he got to the marina, and he had a forty-five-minute to an hour's head start on his parents. . . . He probably got a ride pretty quickly. He's young, looks non-threatening, someone probably gave him a ride. Are they worried that some weirdo might have picked him up?"

"They don't know what to think," she said, sounding exasperated.

"Have they tried the police?"

"Karen said the police told her that because he's over sixteen, he can legally leave home and live on his own." Amanda was slumped over, her elbows in her lap and her head in her hands. "If he was under sixteen they might qualify for an Amber Alert, but for him they'd have to wait forty-eight hours to get any police attention." She looked up at me. "You have to help me find him."

"Me?" That took me by surprise. "I don't even know him! Where would I even begin to look?"

"You were able to find his friend last week," she said. "His parents hadn't even heard of that girl, but you found her."

"You told them about her? Oh, God!" I put my head in my hands.

"They have nowhere to go with this," she said. "Karen is with the police now, trying to get them to do something, but even if they do, it will be a passive search. They won't actively look for him, they're just too busy. The chances of them finding him are slim to none." She had stopped talking. I looked up from my hands, ready to make excuses, but she was crying. Her grey eyes were filled with tears, which she was trying to stop. "I'm sorry," she said, pulling a packet of tissues from her pocket. "This wouldn't have happened if I hadn't stuck my oar in. I should have shut my mouth with Karen, and I shouldn't have pulled you into this mess. You're right. It's too much." Then she got up and headed for the door. "Thanks for the coffee," she said over her shoulder as she reached for the doorknob. She paused at the door, her hand on the knob as I saw her head droop in defeat.

I don't know if it was her crying, or the way she sounded disappointed in me that clinched it, but against what I felt, I said, "Okay, let's start with the Dragon Lady."

Chapter 7

Last week, in my Web search for information about Kyle, I also learned the Dragon Lady's name is Megan. Sometimes she is called Meeker, according to her Facebook page. I was hoping Amanda and I would catch her at her apartment. It was still relatively early in the morning, so if she had slept there last night, she would still be there. If we were lucky, we would catch her before she left for the day. Her street wasn't far from my own, just a few blocks over, so we walked there.

"Unless you have any other ideas, I think we should keep this relaxed when we see her," I suggested. "Let's try not to ring any alarm bells."

"You think she might keep anything she might know from us?" asked Amanda.

"I have a feeling that if Megan thought Kyle was in any trouble she might clam up. The trick is to make her feel at ease," I said. "So that if she says anything, she won't think herself a snitch."

"Don't you think she'll willingly tell us anything she knows?" asked Amanda. "Isn't she a part of the Sticker Generation? I've read that they all crave praise, a pat on the head and a gold star."

"Maybe, but they have a split personality," I replied. "They certainly want the praise, and without any requirement of duty, effort or work, but they also fancy themselves as rebels and tough guys in front of their friends. My God they're obstinate. I've had the displeasure of working with a few lately. I've watched a few get fired, too. They think actors should resemble the movie stars they see in films and TV, or worse, like the petty celebrities in the gossip sheets."

Amanda laughed. "I know. They use the celebs as an aspiration group. I've worked with a few on stage. They refuse to take direction, and sniff at character notes."

"I watched one have a tantrum over a bit of stage business," I added as we walked. Stage business is minor action that actors perform to give depth to a character and add dramatic effect. It's usually not written into the script and is generally small everyday action that people would take for granted, like drumming fingers, or checking the bottom of a shoe when coming in from outside, or licking a finger to smooth out your eyebrows.

"One morning in rehearsal," I continued, "the director had asked this young, would-be superstar to do a bit of stage business. He wanted him to pick up a picture from a table and with a flourish, drop it into a garbage can on stage. The superstar apprentice refused to do it, saying that he didn't feel his character would do that. It soon escalated and became a power struggle between the apprentice and the director. The director, who wouldn't, and couldn't, be undermined by an apprentice in front of the whole company, finally said, 'Just do it, please.'

'No,' said the apprentice flatly, and crossed his arms. 'I can't.'

'All right,' said the director, sounding defeated. 'You are correct. You don't have to do it.' He waited a good five seconds before adding, 'Because the actor who is replacing you will do it. Get out.' The director then turned to the stage manager and said, 'We'll need a replacement here this afternoon. Please bring me the list.'

The apprentice stood on the stage looking shocked while the stage manager called out, 'Fifteen minutes, please!' We cleared the rehearsal hall in record time. The apprentice was gone when we returned."

Amanda roared with laughter.

This generation would flout authority when in a group, and avoid the appearance of complicity with the law, whatever that law was: legal, academic, or parental. So, I was hoping we would find Megan alone; we might have a better chance of getting some information if there was no one else there to play up for.

Amanda and I stood outside Megan's apartment door on the third floor. There was a single pair of black leather flats at our feet. I tapped on the wooden door using the tiny doorknocker in what I hoped was a non-threatening way. I stood back to give her some space when she opened it, but hung close enough to jam my foot in it if she decided to slam it. I put my hands in my pockets to look relaxed and comfortable, to put her at ease. No answer.

"I guess no one's home," I shrugged my shoulders at Amanda. She stepped forward and pounded on the door with the side of her fist. The little doorknocker bounced with every beat. "That's some punch you have there. Been working out?"

"I think I heard some movement in there," she said, and pounded again.

"Yeah, yeah," was the muffled voice from within, as I heard rhythmic shuffling of loose slippers coming toward the door.

Amanda pounded again. "Let's get her attention," smiled Amanda. Megan must have been right there when Amanda hit it the last time, because the lock clicked open immediately. The door opened and a completely different Megan than I had seen last week stood before us. Her straight brown hair was in a neat ponytail, she wore fluffy blue slippers, pink flannel pajamas, and an open, white, terrycloth housecoat. There was no evidence of the tattoo pastiche I had the pleasure to have studied. Her face was screwed up tight to let in as little light as possible.

"Good morning, Megan," I said cheerily. "Late night?"

"Uh, yeah," she said with a voice like a gravel road. "Who're you and what do you want?"

"You may not remember me," I said trying to smile brightly. "I was here last week, looking for Kyle."

She squinted up at me. "Yeah? . . . Oh, yeah . . . I think I remember you," she breathed, emitting a heavy alcohol-and-garlic laden cloud between us. "What do you want?"

"We're looking for Kyle," said Amanda sharply.

"Again? He's probably asleep at home, like the last time," came her sardonic retort, punctuated with a fuzzy interrogative — that lilting and annoying tail end to adolescent girls' speech where the voice rises, just slightly. Megan was no longer an adolescent, but obviously she felt the sarcastic quality gave her statement more weight.

"Not this time," I said. "Have you seen him?"

"Not since last night," she yawned.

"What time was he here?" Amanda asked.

"He wasn't here," said Megan, her eyes shifting up and to the right as if double-checking her answer. "I don't think so, anyway." She scratched her hip through the housecoat. "He was at the party, though. It was late, maybe three or four o'clock."

"Where was the party?" I asked.

"On Spadina, somewhere. I don't remember. Oh yeah, it was the rave."

"Was he still there when you left?"

"I don't know," she whined, putting her fist to her eye like an infant. "There were a lot of people there. He wasn't making any friends though. He was trying to do some business in a place that wasn't his patch." She shook her head like she was trying to shake off the sleepiness. "What time is it?"

"About ten thirty," Amanda said.

"What do you mean, *not his patch*?" I asked. "Was he selling drugs?" Amanda looked at me as if I had said something ridiculous. I had hit it on the head though. It turned out Kyle was selling dope at a squat party, Special K as Megan called it. That wouldn't please his folks. I had no idea what Special K was, but I would look that up later. She let us know that he'd just set up shop, soliciting business. At seventeen I wondered if he was enterprising, brave, or just stupid. Megan hadn't seen him leave, but she didn't remember seeing him when she left, either, so he could have been gone by then. She did admit that she didn't remember much about when she left. She absently reached into her housecoat pocket for a ringing cellphone and flipped it open. She began to read the text on the screen, but she winced at it and gave her head a small shake. She looked like she was trying to decode the message, but her sleep-addled brain wouldn't take in the information.

"I need to know where that party was," I said, trying to bring her attention back to us.

"Maybe I still have the flyer," she conceded, groaning. I thought she was going to shut the door. It started to swing shut so I discreetly placed my foot in the threshold again, but she was just reaching around the back of the door to get at a jacket hanging there. She scooped a small wrinkled flyer out of the pocket and passed it to Amanda. "Okay?' she asked in a tone that said she had had enough. I could tell she wanted to get back to bed, but she sighed as she started to tap out a message on her phone.

I wanted to jangle her a bit more so I said, "How is the Suicide Girls thing going?"

"I . . . How do you know about that?" She stopped typing on the phone. She was clearly rattled, yet pleasantly surprised. Her eyes widened enough that I could see they looked like little road maps. "Did you recognize me from the site? Did you vote for me?"

"Sorry, no," I shook my head. "I was here the night you were shooting the pictures."

"Really? Whoa, I was so out of it that night," she trailed off as her phone beeped again and she absent-mindedly let go of the door.

"Get some sleep," called out Amanda. As Megan slammed the door, the little door knocker bounced.

Here I was, standing outside Megan's apartment building again, this time with Amanda. On my first trip here, I hadn't noticed the debris on the front lawn of the building. There were assorted rusty car parts, beer bottles, a once-wet and now swollen phone book, and an open condom wrapper. There was a small, lone, fencepost by the sidewalk with a stripped bicycle frame locked to it. Even the bike chain was gone. The lawn itself was a hard, grey, dusty patch of ground with one single tuft of grass in the middle. The summer had been unkind to this lawn.

Amanda and I summed up what we knew. We had at least determined that Kyle wasn't out in the wilderness fighting off the fauna while trying to make his way home. "Well, we know he made it back to Toronto last night." I mused aloud. "His parents will be happy to hear that. What will not go over so well with them, is that he was at a rave and hard at work selling drugs."

"Megan said it was a party," said Amanda.

"It was a rave. No one makes a flyer for a party in an industrial area; this is a commercial venture."

"What are you talking about?" asked Amanda.

"These raves aren't like house parties; they're organized by a team," I said. "It's a business. They charge an entrance fee, sell liquor at outrageous prices and sometimes snack foods. The longer people stay, the more they drink, and the more money the organizers make."

"Sounds like one of the clubs on King Street," she said.

"Right, except raves are illegal, unlicensed and they peddle dope," I continued. "I have heard the music is fantastic, and the people are outrageous and fun to watch.

"Okay, we have to involve his parents, now," I said to Amanda. "Give your buddies Karen and Rob a call and let's meet them close to the site of this rave. We can all go in together and then they can take it from there." We boarded the Harbord bus to head toward Spadina Avenue. With any luck, someone might still be there.

We hopped off the Spadina streetcar and stopped in at a Starbucks across the street from the building that housed the rave to make a last-ditch effort to reach Kyle's parents.

"There's still no answer," said Amanda as she popped her phone back into her jacket pocket. "I left her a voice mail, but I didn't tell her any details. I just asked her to phone me." If we didn't make a move soon, there would likely be no one left to ask about Kyle, if there was anyone still there now. Almost half my Saturday was gone, and I didn't want this to drag on any longer than it had to. Of course, if I had been left alone this morning, I would probably still have been asleep anyway.

"Okay, we can't wait any longer or we'll miss our chance. Let's see if anybody is home," I said standing up. We left the Starbucks to head across the street.

Spadina is among the busiest streets in Toronto. The northern area houses the University of Toronto, to the east of Spadina is Chinatown, to the west is Kensington Market, and the south end, the fashion and design district, is where many cultures and neighbourhoods converge. On a Saturday morning, it seems as if half of all humanity is walking there. The other half is driving there. Spadina is very wide and the traffic lights are complex; some are set for cars and others are set for streetcars. They also seem to be timed so that you can't walk across in one go — you have to run.

Amanda and I were at the lower end of Spadina, a few blocks from the lakeshore, looking up at an old eight-storey industrial brick building, probably a remnant from the days when this was the country's garment and fashion hub. We had to circle the building to find a way in. Not surprisingly, the front door was locked, but at the rear there was a large delivery door left wide open. A white unmarked van was parked there half filled with some very large, filthy, plastic storage boxes and green garbage bags. It looked like someone was moving the garbage out.

Amanda looked at the flyer. "Seventh floor: take the freight elevator at the rear," she read. The freight elevator was in use, probably by the guys moving the garbage out.

It struck me as we climbed the first flight of stairs that we didn't have a picture of Kyle. We were going to need one. There was no way these people would remember him from any description I was going to give. I had never met him and had only seen a scratchy unfocussed picture of him on Facebook. I didn't even know his height.

We were halfway up the seven flights when I heard the elevator pass us going the other way. I used the opportunity to take a break from the climb.

"We need a picture," I said, trying not to sound winded. "If his parents had come they could have brought one, but they can never get here in time now. It sounds like these guys are moving out. They'll probably be completely gone in an hour." I had an idea. "What kind of phone do you have?"

"An iPhone," said Amanda. She read my thoughts and was already pulling it out of her pocket to call up Facebook. She had his picture on the screen in no time and we resumed hoofing it upstairs as we heard the elevator start again and head back up.

We opened the stairway door on the seventh floor just as the freight elevator arrived. The elevator door rumbled open, splitting in the middle horizontally like a large mouth. Two brawny guys with a hand truck swung up the cage safety door and emerged staring at us suspiciously. One had a mullet and the other had a porn 'stash. The mullet guy clicked his tongue and gave a wink at Amanda.

"Charming," murmured Amanda. They didn't look like they were in charge so we followed them through some scratched-up, rust-coloured double doors into a cavernous space that took up the whole floor of the building. The floors were wide plank hardwood and must have been original. They were still in relatively good shape, although, they were dirty from last night. I was hoping as we walked over the sticky floor, that the stains were from drinks and nothing more. The ceiling must have been seven metres high with about a dozen industrial ceiling fans. One of the fans had a large mirror ball hanging underneath it, and there were two Klieg lights suspended at either end of the room, pointed at the mirror ball. The space was surrounded on three sides with huge windows, although some of them were covered with large black plywood panels I presumed to mask the lights of the party from showing outside at night and alerting the police. There were easily thousands of beer cans piled in large boxes in a corner. Someone was noisily putting them through a mangle to flatten, so they could pack them more efficiently. The plastic boxes were like the ones I had seen in the van downstairs. The two men we met exiting the elevator were loading the boxes of flattened cans onto the hand dolly to transport them to than van. There was a guy in the far corner standing in front of a long counter that could have served as a bar, making notes in a book. He looked like he was measuring the levels on some liquor bottles. That had to be the boss. He looked up briefly, when we walked into the large room, and then turned his attention back to his book, while we made our way across the floor toward him. He was surely sizing us up as we approached. He was young, in his late twenties, clean-shaven and casually dressed, but obviously not dressed for doing any of the manual labour.

"Good morning," he said cordially as he swung his gaze up to meet us. "How can I help you?"

"We're looking for someone that was here last night," I said. Amanda held up the picture on her iPhone uncomfortably close to his face.

"Never seen him," said the boss. He had hardly looked at the picture, choosing to look Amanda in the eye instead.

"Were you here last night?" asked Amanda in a clipped manner that surprised me. She had lowered her voice a few tones and was pulling the little black notepad out of her pocket that she used to take notes at rehearsal. She flipped to the middle of the pad and began scratching away in it. He didn't answer her. "What's your name?" she added quickly.

"Steve Angeli." He paused, then, "Am I under arrest?" Oh God! He thought we were the police.

"Let's just keep this casual, for now," said Amanda. "A-N-G-E-L-I?" she spelled.

"Yeah," he said a little shaken.

"I thought so," nodded Amanda slowly, keeping her head down and looking at him from beneath furrowed eyebrows. God, she was good. "Now think again. Was he here?" She said each word distinctly for emphasis and held up the picture again.

"Look, there are a lot of people here at night. I can't remember everyone." He was struggling to keep his tone casual.

"Let me refresh your memory," I threw in. I figured it was about time I joined the show. "He might have set up shop peddling Special K." He hesitated looking back and forth between us. He knew something, but he was keeping tight-lipped. "Look, we can do this here, or we can go for a ride and make it official," I added. I was pushing my luck.

"Okay, okay. There was a guy — and he was selling K. I didn't see him, but he was asked to leave."

"Asked to leave?" I said.

"He was, uh, shown the door. Someone told me later that he was pretty mouthy and so, they had to be a little more convincing."

"Was he conscious when he got outside?" asked Amanda.

"I can't say. It wasn't my business. The responsibilities here are very separate. He was stepping on someone else's toes and they aren't very forgiving. They might have taken him for a ride. They've done that before." He made a face that told me it wouldn't have been a pleasure trip.

"Can we talk to these guys?" Amanda fired back.

"Sure, they'll probably be back tonight, but don't ask me to point them out. I'm already sticking my neck out way too far just talking to you. Is this going to go against me?" His cool veneer was beginning to crack.

"We're not interested in your business here, Steve. We need to pick this guy up for something else," I said. "Who are we looking for tonight?"

"Cal," he said quietly, looking around to see if anyone was listening. "Cal will know. He showed him the door." I stood looking at him for a few seconds, in case he wanted to add something. He just stared back at us.

"We may be in touch again," I warned as we left him.

We didn't exchange a word until we were out of sight of the building. We decided to keep alive the illusion that Steve Angeli had created for himself, in the event we needed it again. We headed up Spadina in case we were being watched, so they wouldn't see that we hadn't arrived in a car. The police don't arrive by streetcar, as we did. And I was sure we would certainly be watched as we left.

"Well, we can't very well go back in there tonight," I said to Amanda as we walked. "What made you decide to play Cops and Robbers? That was brilliant, and brave."

"I didn't decide," she said. "He did. I just played along. God, that was exciting!"

Chapter 8

We had nowhere to go from here. The Cal thing was a dead end, or so we thought. We still needed to get in touch with Kyle's parents to share what we had discovered about their son's whereabouts. Even if we decided to pursue Cal, we would have to wait until tonight when he would show up at the rave, and raves start very late. I was eager to wrap this up, but it was already noon and we still didn't know exactly where Kyle was.

Amanda's phone rang while we stood at a street car stop. Once she put it to her ear, all she was able to say for the longest time was *hello*. There was a steady stream of talk coming from the other end. She kept trying to interject with no success.

"Who's that?" I asked "Hamlet?"

Karen she mouthed at me, while I could hear what sounded like someone who wouldn't take a breath. I motioned for her to hand me the phone, which she did, surprisingly. Amanda's expression told me she didn't think there would be an opening in Karen's rant any time soon.

"Karen!" I yelled into the phone. Karen stopped talking. "I want you to let Amanda speak." Then I handed the phone back.

"Masterfully done," she said holding her thumb over the microphone hole. "She's very upset, you know."

She didn't tell Karen much, except that she had been looking for Kyle and she had some help. Amanda told her it would be better to talk face to face. She told me that when Karen was upset, she tended to interrupt your explanation with questions and hijack your train of thought, and compromise your message. Amanda told Karen to meet us at the Boulevard Café. It was central and we needed to eat anyway. In the time it would take her to reach us, Amanda and I could come up with a plan to share our troubling news.

We knew there wouldn't be many more warm days like this to enjoy before winter struck this year, so we decided to sit outside on the patio at the Boulevard. We found a spot close to the sidewalk and each ordered something to eat.

"How the hell are we going to find this Cal, and frankly, do we even want to?" I was thinking out loud. "If he is the guy that forcibly removed Kyle from the party, he may not be disposed to answering questions. We got lucky with Steve this morning, but we can't count on fooling anybody else. If we could get to Cal before he goes on duty tonight, maybe, but we don't know anything else about him. I guess it really doesn't matter anyway. Once your friends Karen and Rob get here, we can give them the info and hand off this mess to them." I was just starting to realize the weekend was still within my grasp, when Amanda sat up in her seat and craned her neck to look over my shoulder.

"Isn't that your little friend?" she said, pointing behind me with her sandwich. I swung around to look. Megan, wearing a small silver backpack, big sunglasses, and a white ball cap with her ponytail sticking out at the back, was walking along Harbord Street toward the university and us.

She was deep in her own thoughts, and I think I startled her when I spoke. "Hello Megan." She stopped dead and looked back and forth between Amanda and me for a few seconds before making a connection.

"Oh it's you, again. You guys are starting to creep me out. Are you, like, stalking me?" She looked much more wide awake now as she pulled her sunglasses off and squinted at us in the sunlight.

"We've been sitting here for the best part of a half-hour; we're almost finished lunch. Does it make sense that we're stalking you?" Amanda replied. Megan just stared at her. "Maybe you can help us, though," Amanda went on. "Who's Cal?"

"Cal who?" Megan held her hand up to shield her eyes, instead of putting her sunglasses back on.

"Cal from the rave place," said Amanda.

"Oh, Cal. . . . He's the doorman. He's huge," she said making the word even sound large. "He works out at the university gym every day. He has a job at the rave to help pay for school."

"He works out every day?" I asked. "When?"

"He's always there," she shrugged. "You would have to always be there, to look like that."

"What does he look like?" asked Amanda.

We got his description after some prodding, and I excused myself to walk the few blocks to the university athletic centre, leaving Amanda and Megan to chat. Now that she was wide awake, there was a possibility we could get more information from her. Amanda would wait for Karen, and of course, she offered to pick up the cheque. I didn't plan it; that's just the way it worked out.

Megan had proven to be a valuable resource. People like her are always looking for information and storing it away in case they need it again. They trade information, their currency, for influence and control, as they climb their power ladder. For some reason, Megan seemed to think we could further her cause, whatever that was, so she gave us information. They were chatting away as I left them: Amanda in her seat, and Megan standing on the sidewalk, resting her elbows on the patio railing.

Saturday at noon, I discovered, is the perfect time to go to the university gym. It is virtually empty except for the staff and diehard fitness freaks. Even the staff members are hard to find. I breezed through the turnstile at the front entrance without seeing anyone. I got lucky and found Cal, despite Megan's description, which was way off the mark, except for his size. He wasn't as tall as she said, and his hair was much shorter. He also didn't look as mean, though he was, indeed, huge—a mountain of muscle. I found him in the free-weights room where he was taking a break between sets. He was sweaty, leaning on a rack of dumbbells and drinking a thick milkshake-like substance out of a shaker the size of a pail. Every time he took a sip, it left a wide milky moustache.

"You're Cal!" I said smiling as I approached him.

"Guilty!" he responded with his own smile, without knowing what I was about. He wiped off the milk moustache with his small towel that looked like a face cloth in his giant hands.

"You were working at the rave last night," I said, maintaining a friendly smile. He stretched his pectorals, which stressed the fabric of his black T-shirt to nearly tearing. "You handled that guy pretty well."

"Which guy? There were a lot of assholes last night," he said.

"That's why they need talent like you," I said trying to compliment. "I mean the Special K kid."

"Oh, him. Well, he was easy. He's been in before and he's been asked to leave before. He's a mouthy little puke, but he didn't give me any real trouble. He was bitching the whole time, but I couldn't hear him." He shrugged and took another sip of the chalky liquid.

"Music too loud?

"Sort of. I wear earplugs to protect my hearing. So, I don't hear much when the music's going. Once you damage your hearing, it never comes back," he said sounding like a public service announcement. "My dad taught me that. He was on a city road crew, worked the jackhammer. Anyway, all I had to do was get that kid to the door. He was picked up there by the Pack Boys," he said. "They drove off with him." I made a mental note of the Pack Boys.

"What would they want with him?" I probed.

"He was selling K. That's their thing. Well, not just Ketamine, but whatever is on their menu that night." I made another mental note. "They have an agreement with Sal, I think. I don't get involved with that. I just handle the door. They were probably going to put a scare into him, maybe try to find out who was supplying him, and then spook him into staying away. He was cutting into their profit margin. They probably took him to their place on Baldwin. What's your interest in this?" he asked.

"I, uh, have my own spot," I said quickly, wondering how best to extricate myself from this.

"You looking for someone on the door?" he asked brightly, changing the subject for me.

"You're not happy where you are?" I asked him, deflecting.

"This one is at the end of its product life cycle," he said. "It is starting to go too legit and losing its edge, you know. If there's no risk and the clientele starts looking too mainstream, the preferred group stops coming."

"Oh?" I didn't know how to respond to this, but I didn't have to. He continued as if he were teaching a class.

"The first group that comes, when a rave opens, are the artists, musicians, film types, professional athletes — you know the nouveau riche. They are the target market. They have an entourage, lots of cash, and they flaunt their wealth: watches, jewellery, cars, designer clothes, and they only drink the premium brand names, whether it's booze or bottled water. You get the legit club owners coming after hours, because the place gets talked about. Then their wait staff start coming because the celebrities and athletes are there, and everyone wants to be in the company of a superstar. Word spreads, and then the petty criminals start arriving, the hipsters, and *faux-hemians*."

"Who?" I was pretending to follow most of this but he'd just lost me.

"The faux-hemians? Oh, they imitate the look of artsies, but they're pretenders, the tire kickers," he explained. "They have just enough money for the cover, so they nurse one drink all night or worse, bring their own. The bad boys have money, but don't spend it, although, they like to flash it around. I like to watch them pay for a drink and pull out a wad of bills the size of a mortgage. They're just looking to connect and claim some new territory. As the word goes viral, the celebrities feel crowded and gawked at, so they find other places. Soon it's real-estate agents, suburban types, and the last straw is the teenage girls. They look great, but shit, they can't hold their liquor, and there is always someone passing out in the can or crying or puking. As soon as you see the teenage girls arrive in a pack, that's the month you have to fold the tent and move on. I've seen it all before. And the clientele at this place is already starting to migrate. Maybe they're drifting in your direction. So, if you're looking for someone on the door . . ."

"Not yet," I interrupted, trying to keep on top of the conversation. "I'm still building. I'll keep you in mind, though. Can I always reach you here?" I thought I had the information I needed, but I wanted some assurance that I could find him if I needed him again.

"Yeah, I'm here every day, but let me give you my card," he said, which surprised me. He leaned over the weight bench and reached into his bag to pull out what looked like a business card. It had all his contact information but no company name.

"Perfect," I said. "What are you studying here?"

"Business Admin," he said shaking my hand. I made my escape without him even asking my name.

I called Amanda on my way outside to let her know I was on my way back. Karen still hadn't shown up at the Boulevard. The university athletic centre is only a few blocks away and only had to say a few words to her before she came into view sitting on the patio. I filled her in on what I learned from Cal.

"Success!" I said. "Our man Cal was there, and he isn't anything like I imagined."

"Scary?" She asked. I wanted to think it sounded sympathetic, but it didn't.

"No, he was disarmingly friendly, and all business," I said. "He remembers Kyle, too. And he remembers throwing him out, *and* this wasn't the first time, either. He is a bit of a pest by Cal's account. I was under the impression that this was a rave party, but it sounds a lot more like a booze-can."

"You've lost me," she said.

"It's an after-hours bar, only it's illegal, unlicensed," I explained. "It appears that a group of *business people* have come together to provide a place for the glitterati to hang out after hours. The drinks are overpriced, and it is somewhat exclusive."

"So, how does Kyle get into an exclusive bar?" she asked pointedly.

61

"I have no idea, but Cal said that the crowd is starting to evolve, and a less desirable clientele is showing up. However he gets in, they throw him out as soon as they can. Cal said he was handed off to somebody called the Pack Boys. What sounded worse, though, was that they might have taken them to their place on Baldwin Street."

The server was getting impatient with us sitting there. She was hanging around at the edge of the patio with her arms crossed and I swear she was tapping her foot, so I ordered another coffee to keep her from hovering. "What about you?" I asked. "Did you get anything from Megan?"

Amanda had spent quite some time talking to Megan. Megan's primary objective in life, she confided to Amanda, was to be famous. It didn't really matter how, either. She had no plans to do anything that would merit fame, like winning a gold medal at the Olympics, inventing a cure for a disease or becoming a world class singer or actor. Her rationale was that, if she acted famous and hung out in the places the celebs did, people would assume she was famous. Adulation, and of course, money would follow. When Amanda asked her where that money would come from, Megan said product endorsements, and a rich man would marry her to cash in on her fame. There were also commercials. She would do a bunch of commercials, she said.

Nothing makes an actor angrier than to hear someone outside of the business blithely suggest that the actor do a few commercials to make some quick cash, as if they were easy to come by. Commercials are some of the most competitive of all the acting jobs and scarcer than they look. Amanda said that she was weighing a decision to either laugh in her face or smack the kid, when Megan saved herself by continuing to speak.

"Did you tell her that you were an actor?" I asked.

"I could not get a word in," said Amanda. "She just kept yammering on, and using a vocal fry to assert her importance. I swear she sounded like she was running out of air at the end of each sentence, and would expire. She didn't though.

"She told me she had picked a few role models from the rich and famous in the media and determined that if she acted the way they did, within an undetermined amount of time, she too would gain celebrity. She felt that by embracing the same behaviour as the rich, famous and foolish, she too would climb the fame ladder. She didn't call it foolish, though. She used the term *eccentric*." Amanda made air quotes again.

"She had even gone so far as to accept that even though she could not claim any substance on which to build her fame, fame would most certainly come. She didn't put it quite so eloquently," continued Amanda, "but she definitely has big plans and she seems driven to get what she wants. The thing is, she doesn't have anything to lose, really. I think her folks are providing her with a financial safety net, so if she fails, she won't get too bruised."

"Who is she modelling herself after?" I asked.

"Oh she has quite a group of worthies that she is selecting attributes from," said Amanda with a flourish of her hand. "There are some she looks to for clothing and some for the music she listens to. Then there is one for sexual preferences and exploits, which she admits might not be factual because she has only seen reports in the tabloids. There is even one role model for her tattoos. There is a bunch more, but I started to get a bit lost. Most of them I'd never heard of. She is overplanting numerous seeds to see which ones take root and grow. Her prototypes run from anime heroine to biker chick.

"The fact that she is picking what she likes from some and discarding the rest is a bit weird. It's kind of like, you know, when people cherry-pick the rituals from a series of faiths and try to blend them into something easy to follow. That way, they can cast off the distasteful and then they won't have to adhere to what they find inconvenient in their own religion. Like a New Age religion."

"*Newage*," I said, purposely mispronouncing it. "I like it to rhyme with *sewage*. I guess when you can't find something substantial to nourish you, you'll try to live on the crumbs. It was once said, 'Popularity is the very crumbs of greatness.'"

"Ah, Victor Hugo," said Amanda.

"Actually, it was Leonard Nimoy," I said. "But I think he was paraphrasing Hugo. I think it goes beyond New Age religion, though, it's almost like a cargo cult."

"What are you talking about?" asked Amanda, shaking her head.

"A cargo cult."

She made hand motions as if she were directing me into a parking space. I took that to mean she wanted me to elaborate.

"All right, there was a primitive society living on an island in the Pacific Ocean during the Second World War. One of the armies, I can't remember which one, decided to occupy the island as an outpost. So, they set up a base there. They built a runway for planes and a small harbour pier for supply boats to dock and unload. When the local people saw the goods that were brought in — the food, machines, and weapons — they were amazed, and a little jealous. Like many societies, they thought of themselves as the gods' anointed people, and naturally, felt that these goods were really meant for them as gifts. They saw the ships and the planes as messengers from the gods, and these newcomers, the invading army, had wrongfully intercepted their gifts.

"When the occupying army left after the war, the local people waited for the planes and the ships to return with more gifts. They didn't. It only took a while for them to deduce that if they wanted to please the gods, and have the messengers return in the planes, they would have to perform the same rituals and act like the people who attracted the gods in the first place. So, they began marching around and holding sticks over their shoulders, like the army had done with their rifles. When that wasn't enough, they built a replica of the control tower out of sticks and palms. They even built a copy of an airplane out of bamboo and leaves. They kept adding more and more to what they could remember the army had done to bring the gods' messengers back but, of course, the gods' messengers never returned. The islanders assumed they were missing something important in the rituals they were performing. They were missing the substance, but they couldn't know that. They continued this for years, until the reasons for the rituals were forgotten and disappeared. Strangely though, the rituals remained, even until recently. They, in effect, built a cult around the cargo."

"But, they couldn't possibly have known there was any more to it," said Amanda, "because that's all they were exposed to."

"Exactly," I agreed. "And all the public is really exposed to with the celebrities, is what they read and see in the media. Look, if I don't think critically, or I'm not even a bit skeptical, and I repeatedly read in the tabloids that a rich and famous person is acting like an idiot again, I might assume that he is famous because he acts that way."

"That's a bit simplistic, don't you think?" she said.

"For you it is, but there are a lot of folks that don't see beyond what's in their immediate grasp. I see people all the time that believe that other folks' good fortune is really meant for them, even though they have done nothing to earn those rewards. How often do you hear some contemptible person point to someone else's good fortune, or reputation and say, 'That should have been mine,' or 'I deserve that'?"

She nodded and said, "You're right. They make a leap away from good sense; they think there's no need to work to achieve wealth and fame. They are owed to them."

"For some people, it's not that much of a leap, and the media play it up. So do the advertisers, making all kinds of promises without any substance: like weight loss in a pill, happiness in a car, sophistication in a cigarette, even the lotteries."

"So, you're saying, if they just diverted their energy and thought, from the flashy behaviour into something of substance," she said, "they might get closer to achieving what they want. That's a bit preachy."

"But we're all a little guilty of embracing our own version of a cargo cult," I explained. "I think actors, by definition, live very close to it all the time. And to be honest, I am guilty of buying the odd lottery ticket."

Our long-awaited guest, Karen, arrived just as the coffee did, and she wasn't what I had expected. I guess I was anticipating someone who looked like my own mother, or one of my mother's friends. I couldn't have been farther off the mark. Karen was slim, fit, and chic as she slipped out of her shiny black Murano across the street, pausing slightly to check her reflected appearance in the driver's side window. Her expensive jeans and urban hiking boots were topped with a short, light coloured jacket. The jacket sat just high enough to highlight her slim hips and long legs. Her blonde hair was perfectly cut in a bob and she had taken the time to apply makeup before she had left home. She strode confidently across the street merely glancing in either direction, seeming to dare the traffic to come too close to her at their peril. She saw us only as she reached the sidewalk and came directly to Amanda to hug her. To her credit, she didn't kiss Amanda on both cheeks, although I was expecting that, too.

"This is Michael Dion," said Amanda by way of an introduction. "Michael's giving me a hand at looking for Kyle."

"I'm very pleased to meet you. And thank you for helping," Karen said, formally. Then very businesslike asked, "So, where are we?"

"Let's sit," I offered, and ordered her a coffee. I think the server had been expecting us to leave. She rolled her eyes and made a theatrical exit from the patio into the restaurant.

"Is your husband still with the police?" I asked.

"No, Rob is out of town," she said calmly, which took me by surprise. She must have noticed my expression because she continued with an explanation. "He got a call early this morning—in the middle of the night, really. There was an emergency meeting in Ottawa. He had to leave immediately. He was on the six a.m. flight."

"Ottawa?" It came out before I could rein it in.

"What about Kyle?" asked Amanda. "Isn't he worried about Kyle?"

"Rob doesn't think this is serious. He thinks Kyle is just trying to punish us," said Karen, "that he will stay at a friend's place maybe for a few days, and then come home after a while, once he feels we have learned our lesson or he has worn out his welcome there. Rob says he refuses to accommodate Kyle's bullying. He also had no choice. It was an emergency, he had to go."

"But, Ottawa?" I asked again. "How long will he be there?"

"Probably a few days," she said calmly. "Maybe less. It depends on the problem."

"Well, Kyle is in Toronto," I said, coming to our problem. "Somewhere in Toronto, anyway."

"How do you know?" she asked, looking surprised. She turned to Amanda. "Is he a detective?"

"No, I'm an actor. I work with Amanda. Now, there were at least two sightings of your son last night," I informed her. She sat, looking back at me with her face unmoving. I started off slowly to ease into what we knew. I told her about the rave, the dope, and the gang that drove away with him. She dismissed the gang reference as probably just some friends. Even the bit about him selling dope didn't faze her. She was very business-like in her responses, which made me uncomfortable.

"We are going to see what else we can find out," I continued. "Last week, I found out a few things, and only had time to follow up on one before Kyle turned up at home. There were other leads we might check."

"Leads?" said Amanda a little sarcastically. "I thought you were an actor and not a detective."

"I was once in an episode of *Davinci's Inquest*," I said.

"All that from one episode?"

"Yes," I said proudly. "And I was an extra, but I learn fast. Anyway, we'll have to follow where the information we have takes us."

"What do you want me to do?" asked Karen looking at me. She had maintained her level business-like voice, but her eyes were worried.

I had no idea what I wanted her to do, but she seemed to think I was in charge. "Well, we need to find a trail of his movements last night," I began slowly. "He may have been in touch with some of his friends before he went to the rave. He might also have been in touch with someone after the rave, or after he left these Pack Boys. Has Kyle ever mentioned them? Have you ever heard of them?"

Her eyes moved to the right as she shook her head slowly. "No."

"I guess we'll try to contact his friends first then . . . and I may want to look up the Pack Boys, too." I was beginning to get jumpy. Whether it was the excitement or all the coffee, I wanted to start on this and get it finished as soon as possible. My free weekend was starting to get away from me again. "I'm going back to my place," I said. "Amanda, get a list of all of Kyle's friends that Karen can think of. Get as much detail as you can: schools, addresses, workplaces if they have jobs, places they hang out . . . anything at all. I'll start where I left off last week and we'll see if your info can fill in some gaps. Who knows what we can dig up in the next little while? Maybe he'll just show up at home again," I offered lightly. Karen's stone-faced expression was beginning to weaken, so I hastily took my leave and said, "I'll see you back at my place."

Chapter 9

I might have given Karen and Amanda the impression that I had a plan to find Kyle, but I had no idea what I was doing. I am an actor, not a private eye, I reminded myself as I stepped into my apartment. I needed some help. I had just begun to research Ketamine on my computer when the door buzzed. I was surprised that it had taken Amanda and Karen so little time to compile the information we needed about Kyle's friends. I guessed that either Kyle had only a few friends or only a few friends that his parents knew about — not surprising, when they had no idea he was going to raves and peddling Ketamine.

I got up to buzz the door downstairs and returned to the computer while I waited for Amanda and Karen. I heard the door open behind me and launched into what I'd already found.

"It's a veterinary anaesthetic!" I said incredulously. "Vets use Ketamine as a general anaesthetic. He's selling veterinary drugs to people."

"Who is?" came Nigel's voice from behind. I turned just in time to see him open my fridge and start poking around.

"What are you doing here?" I asked. "And let me know if you find anything you like in my fridge."

"Just browsing," he retorted languidly while pulling out a tub of hummus from the fridge. "What's this about veterinary drugs and who were you talking to? How old is this hummus?"

"Try it and see. That kid has gone missing again, the one from last week, and Amanda has enlisted me to help out again," I said turning back to my research. "Anyway, this kid has been going out to raves on the weekends and selling Ketamine."

"Special K?" queried Nigel, lobbing the hummus into the garbage after a sniff. "Hallucinations, flashbacks, muscle spasms, that crap's unpredictable — not the hummus, the Ketamine."

"You've heard of it?" I spun round to look at him.

"Of course," he shrugged. "So, why does that make you talk to yourself?" He had found a bag of baby carrots and began to devour them noisily.

"Amanda is on her way over now. I thought you were her." I strolled over to the fridge, reached in and handed him a tub of ranch dip for the carrots. The cat had come out of hiding and began to purr loudly and wrap around Nigel's leg while I went back to the laptop to see what else I could find.

"What's going on with this cat?" he asked with an eyebrow arched in concern. The cat was howling and circling his leg with wanton intent. He had lowered his voice a fifth for effect. "I think she has a cross-species attraction issue."

"She's in heat," I confessed sheepishly. I braced myself for what was coming.

"I thought you were getting her spayed!"

"I was going to, but I didn't have the money. I started to save for it," I began to explain. Nigel's face told me he wasn't buying it. "By the time I had enough money, she was *in season*, as they say."

"Why not do it now?" he asked accusingly.

"Vets don't like to operate when cats are . . . like this," I explained pointing an accusing finger at the cat, "so, they charge more. I don't have quite that much money saved yet."

"It seems cruel to leave her like this," he said wincing. "It's entertaining though. She sounds a bit like Florence Foster Jenkins."

"She'll give up eventually," I said hopefully. Then, in an effort to distract him, I invited him to look at the computer screen. "Come and see this. This is Megan's Facebook page." I pointed her out to Nigel.

"The Dragon Lady?" he asked. "Oooh! Nice tats."

I had found some pictures in her Facebook photo album. She was in a number of frames, half of which were taken of herself at arm's length, either looking like she was screaming with delight or doing the inevitable pouty kiss at the lens. They lived their lives like it was an eternal frosh week: drinking, taking bits of their clothes off, and endlessly mugging for the ever-present cameras. There were loads of pictures of people taking pictures of people taking pictures, which to me, became some weird, nested abstraction.

"Who are all these people with her?" asked Nigel.

"No idea," I said, "but here is our boy." I put my finger on the screen. Kyle was one of the eight or ten faces in the photo. He stood behind the others.

"That's not a great picture," said Nigel. "He's in the background and a bit out of focus."

"He is in a few more of these," I said, flipping through the frames until I found him again. "He's not featured in any of the pictures, though. He doesn't seem to be a part of the core group."

"You're right," offered Nigel. "He's not even interacting with the main players. He's more like a hanger-on — an extra. Why don't you go to his Facebook page?"

"I tried that. His security settings are set too high for me to get any info. His friends are listed, though, so I was able to go through his friends until I found someone with lower security settings. Then I trolled through their wall messages and pictures until I came up with Kyle."

"That was easy," said Nigel.

"I got lucky. Kyle has hundreds of friends and some of them use aliases or nicknames. I just happened to pick a few of the right people to look into. The deeper I went, I found patterns and their movements became predictable. I simply arranged the pieces to assemble a picture of their public life. Even those using an alias or a nickname were tagged occasionally with their real names."

Nigel and I continued to scroll through the pages. There were hundreds of pictures with similar images, and images of people in dangerous situations like rooftop parties, people standing on train tracks with liquor bottles, running down subway tunnels, holding up bongs or joints or crack pipes, and I'm sure we only scratched the surface. I was making notes and cutting and pasting the names and URLs onto a separate document so I could get back to them easily later. The drawback with tracking on Facebook is that the searches tend to meander, so I knew there was no guarantee I could duplicate a pathway if I needed to.

Nigel's interest shifted as we continued. He went from amused observer to serious commentator, and then he became an irritated critic. "Have you noticed that these kids don't seem to have a real life?" commented Nigel quietly over my shoulder. "I mean, you would think from the pictures they take they exhibit absolutely no responsible behaviour. Even if I give them the benefit of the doubt, and they do act responsibly on occasion, it appears all they do is drink, mug for the camera, and have faux sex. Look at this picture," he pointed to a picture of a girl supine on the ground surrounded by empty beer cans and a liquor bottle. "That girl is unconscious on her back and there is a puddle of vomit by her head." He paused for a beat. "Everyone else in the picture is laughing and ignoring her. She could conceivably have alcohol poisoning." He was positively seething.

We had to stop. There was no use going on until Amanda and Karen arrived with a list of names we could cross-reference with the characters on the Web. I brought Nigel up to speed on the developments so far because my brief research had piqued his curiosity, and I needed a sounding board to organize my thoughts.

"You've had a busy morning," he concluded. "What happens from here?"

"I'll see if the list of names that Amanda gets from Karen is any help. That's probably the best place to start. I really don't want to go back to the rave again tonight. The bartender, or whatever he was, Steve, thinks we're the police, and the bouncer thinks I have a club of my own. I don't want to risk being recognized or remembered from this morning. Just imagine if they exchanged notes and got conflicting stories.

"I thought Steve was the boss, but the bouncer I met at the gym, Cal, mentioned someone named Sal who had given the Pack Boys permission to open their franchise there. So Sal must be the boss."

"We can do a search on him," said Nigel. "We may get lucky."

"It won't do me any good," I said. "I can't go back to the rave again without blowing my cover."

"They've never seen *me* though," Nigel grinned. "I could have a look."

"You cannot go in there. We don't know what they're capable of."

"We won't know if we don't try," he said. "I've got nothing else on for tonight. We can quickly build me a character, and I'll try to find out something. I don't have to actually *do* anything. I'll just walk around, have a drink, enjoy the music and scenery, and gather intelligence. It's worth a try." The door buzzed.

"That will be Amanda and Karen," I said while going over to the button to buzz them in. I tripped over the cat who shrieked and ran under the couch. "We'll see what kind of info they bring us."

Amanda arrived alone and was a bit amazed to see Nigel there. "Nigel! This is a surprise."

"I just stopped in for a snack," he said holding up the empty carrot bag. "But Michael has been telling me about your adventure this morning, and I am ready to go to the rave tonight, *undercover*."

Amanda didn't even hesitate. "Perfect," she said.

So we added Nigel to the crew. I wanted to know what happened to Karen.

"She went home," Amanda said, "in case Kyle shows up there to either stay or pack his things."

"Has she tried to phone him?" Nigel asked. "I'm sure he must have a cellphone."

"Yeah, an iPhone," said Amanda. "His mother threw it into a lake last night. That's the spark that lit the tinder."

"I thought she threw his iPod into the lake," I said.

"An iPhone is also an iPod," explained Amanda, pointedly.

I briefed Amanda on what we had just found on the Web and Nigel volunteered again to go deep under cover, as he put it. Amanda embraced the idea and was all for helping to build the subtext for a character for him to give him a way of behaving once he was there, so he wouldn't look suspicious. It would also provide him with a cover story if he was approached and someone tried to strike up a conversation. We couldn't take the risk of people making up their own story, as they had done with Amanda and me earlier in the day. We were lucky that their imaginations travelled in the same direction as our objective. Nigel decided it was best to try to make them uneasy. His idea was to play a dangerous-looking character.

"But you'll go in and be quiet," I said. "You'll keep away from the sides of the room; always walk through the centre to assert dominance. Take your time with everything; moving slowly will make you look confident and powerful." I could see Nigel slipping the character on as we went through it. "Look around a bit, like you're admiring the place at first, but don't look too impressed."

"Next you'll have me pissing on the chairs to mark my territory," he said, and then he paused thoughtfully. "Oh, right . . . Okay, I get this. Make it look like I could own the place. I'll order a drink — either soda water or Grey Goose."

"Right," I said, "Soda . . . Perrier would be too pretentious. Grey Goose is just right." Then, I thought aloud, "The only thing better is if you order a Grey Goose first and they have none, so in a disappointed tone, you ask for a soda instead."

"Oh, God, that would be priceless!" laughed Nigel.

"What the hell are you two up to?" interjected Amanda. "This is no joke. There is a boy who might be in danger here."

"A very stupid boy, who sells drugs, but you're right," I said. "All right, we need a way to extract information from these guys to lead us to where Kyle might be or where they might have taken him. They're not going to just tell us if we ask them. We're going to have to somehow convince them to offer us the information." I turned to Nigel. "How tough are you going to be?"

"I am thinking about having only one scar," he said thoughtfully, "a small one, but on my face."

76

"What about on your neck, instead?" Amanda jumped in. "A scar on the neck would be masked a bit so that would be more mysterious and cover any imperfections of the makeup."

"Imperfections? In my makeup? You're joking of course," said Nigel. Then he asked, "Knife wound or rope burn?"

"Knife," said Amanda decisively. "A rope mark means you've been attacked and bound. A knife wound may mean you were in a fight and won."

"A recent scar? Pink and angry looking?" he mused.

"No, an old scar is better," said Amanda. "A recent scar would mean there was a recent power struggle, and you might still be engaged in it — weakens the character. An old scar means that even though there might have been a clash, it was a long time ago and suggests you are still top dog. Also, a pink scar would be too distracting. You can't look at a recent scar and not help but wonder how painful it is."

"Still, you must always juxtapose your dangerous persona with a calm, confident, and genteel demeanor," I reminded him, as if I were giving a note to an actor. "Quiet is much more threatening. Your objective," I continued, "is to get as much info on this kid as possible. Maybe the kid owes you money." Nigel nodded. "And don't drive there in your car. You don't want them taking down your plate number. Take a cab. You have a suitable wardrobe?"

He assured us he had just the thing. I was relieved by how seriously he was taking this. "I'll call you when I leave the place," he said. "It will be late, but we should meet here to compare notes afterward. In the meantime, if you find out anything about this Sal character, call me. Remember, I'm going in blind, so any additional information will be helpful." I gave him the address for the rave and he left to prepare.

I turned to Amanda. "OK, so what have you brought?" She pulled out a handwritten list. There were three names I recognized from the searches I had done earlier. We started looking on the Web again. Only one of the new names came up consistently in the pictures at the rave or other dodgy looking places. Our friend, Megan, was featured in many of them, too. Eventually, we came across a section with references to the Pack, or the Pack Boys, or just the Boys. There were a few pictures of people going in the front door of an old house at night. The caption under one photo read Baldwin. I remembered that Steve at the rave site said the Pack Boys had a place on Baldwin Street. We tried to make out the number on the front of the house in the picture, but it was obscured by a shadow. Baldwin isn't a long street so I thought I would take a bus ride over to walk by the house and have a look; nothing more.

"I'm going with you," said Amanda.

Chapter 10

There was ample time to turn around and head back to my apartment. I could have had a nice dinner, studied my script, and gone to bed early. I could have gone to the weekend animal clinic and inquired about spaying the cat, maybe even tried to negotiate the price down, but I did none of that. Instead, I stood at the door of the Pack Boys' house on Baldwin, thinking I could get them to tell me what happened to that idiot boy who was muscling in on their territory the night before.

The house was easy enough to find. It looked just like the picture on the website, except the picture didn't do justice to the eight square metres of hard-packed grassless front yard and the grey paint that was cracked and peeling in large curls off the wooden steps and handrail. The house was in a residential neighbourhood, so I mistakenly thought that there was no risk in knocking on the door and asking a few questions.

We agreed that Amanda would wait discreetly at the corner, a few houses away beside a light pole, while I approached the house. On the way to the front door, I walked past a hopped up, Honda Civic with medium-blue paint, acid-green wheels and almost blacked out tinted windows. The house looked ready to fall down, while the car parked on the parking pad was pristine. I could easily imagine the sound of the stereo thumping out of the car when it was running.

I realized too late that I banged on the door a bit too hard, although, I couldn't have known what I would encounter. The guy who answered the door looked like someone out of a comic strip. He was so skinny his tight black jeans and black T-shirt made him look malnourished. His head was tilted to the right and back a bit, and his lips were pursed as if he had just been surprised by a lemon between his teeth. His obviously dyed, jet-black hair stood straight up from his head giving the effect that he was a living, breathing exclamation point. With a squint in his eyes, he looked me up and down. I'm sure he felt his facial contortions made him look powerful. He said nothing; he just stared at me.

This will be easy, I thought. Unless he doesn't speak English.

"Hello," I began, pleasantly. "I am looking for someone. He may have come here last night." He still said nothing, nor did he move, but he exhaled quickly and loudly through his nose, which I took as an indication that he at least heard me.

"His name is Kyle," I continued. "He was at the big rave on Spadina. I think he came here after."

"Fuck off," he said quietly, yet clearly. Well, he spoke English. He then swung the door to close it. I was ready for that though, and slipped my foot in the threshold to stop it dead. He looked at me for a second and then turned and walked into the house, leaving the door to slowly swing back open. Naturally, I followed him in and was about to threateningly ask him if there was anyone else here that I could talk to, but I didn't get the chance. I felt a sudden crashing pain on the back of my skull and watched helplessly as the floor quickly rose up to meet my face.

80

When I opened my eyes, I was a bit disoriented. It took a few moments for my eyes to focus and the heavy feeling to leave my limbs. Strangely, I was looking at a blue, cloudless sky as my face tingled and felt as though the blood was making its way back into it. I had no idea where I was. The base of my skull throbbed horribly and I couldn't manage to get up or move at all. I gradually became aware of the smell of rubber and gasoline and soon realized why. As I became able to move my aching head, I raised it to see that the lower part of my body was buried in old tires and I was wet. The smell told me that I had been liberally sprinkled with gasoline. I urgently looked around, fearing I would find an open flame, but there was no flame, thank God, and not a soul in sight. There was an old leaky gas can on its side next to me, balancing on a tire, with gas trickling out of it onto the tire that lay across my hip. I heaved the tire and the gas can away. I recalled that I had gone to a Baldwin Street building, that Amanda came with me, and that I went into the house. My memory stopped once I had asked about Kyle. Then it came to me: this was a warning to walk away. As the sense of immediate danger settled, my field of vision broadened, and I discovered that I was in a back alley between rows of houses. It was still light out, so I couldn't have been unconscious for very long. I struggled to pull myself up from under the weight of the tires, looking both ways for an escape route. Although I was light-headed, I walked quickly, and unsteadily, toward the closest end of the alley. As the dizziness left me, my legs became steadier, so I attempted to run toward the safety of the street. The end of the alley turned and emptied onto Baldwin with a sight that was pleasantly familiar: the back side of Amanda. She was still standing at the corner behind a tree craning her neck, looking away from me and toward the house. I slowed as I came up behind her. I was about to reach up and tap her shoulder when my cellphone rang. She swung around as I answered it, making a face and recoiling at the smell of me.

"Hello?" I said into the phone. I held up my hand to let Amanda know I would be right with her.

"Michael, it's Brandi," said my agent. I could hear that she had a cigarette in her mouth. "I've got something for you."

"A job?" My head was pounding, but this was good news. I rubbed the back of my aching head.

"An audition," she said exhaling what I imagined was a cloud of smoke.

"Stratford or Shaw?" I said facetiously.

"Don't make me laugh with Stratford or Shaw. I don't make enough money on those. This is a commercial . . . national, too," she said enthusiastically. "Wednesday. Are you up for it?"

"Of course. Email me the details," I said. "I'm out right now, but I'll call you as soon as I can."

After I had folded my phone and slipped it into my pocket, I looked up to see Amanda looking incredulously at me. Her arms were stretched wide to either side and her mouth was open. "What the hell is going on?"

"That was my agent," I said. "I have an audition for a commercial on Wednesday."

"I watched you go into that house twenty minutes ago," she said, pointing down the street. "Then you show up behind me on the phone, booking auditions and smelling like . . . what *is* that smell?"

"Gas."

"Gas? What happened in the house? What did you find out?"

"I don't know, and nothing. They clobbered me and threw me into the alley before burying me in tires and dousing me with gas." I rubbed the back of my head. I could feel a bump rising.

"What?" she said, exasperated. "There's blood on your hand!"

"That's just from my head where someone hit me," I said looking at the blood spot on my fingertip. "Let's get out of here, before they see you with me. Let's keep your face out of this for now."

"No! I think you have to go back and force the issue," she said, suddenly sounding like a guidance counsellor talking about bullies. "If they think we're afraid of them, we'll never find out what happened to Kyle. I think this proves they know what happened to him or they know where he is."

My phone rang again. I reached into my pocket for it and Amanda snatched it away before I could open it.

"Let it go to voice mail," she said hotly. "It'll keep until you get back. Now go!" She pointed in the direction of the house.

I had always thought she was sensible, and that is what probably helped to cloud my judgment. I still thought that when this was all over, I had a chance with her, especially since she was beginning to treat me with contempt. Women usually wait until they start dating me before they treat me that way; maybe I thought it was a sign she was headed in that direction. But it was probably because I was still fuddled after the smash on the head, or the influence of the gasoline fumes that allowed me to be persuaded to make my way back to that front door again. If I had thought about it, and paid more attention to the growing lump on the back of my head, I would have demurred.

The door was just as I remembered it, but this time I decided I would be less assertive when knocking. I tapped the door lightly and surprised the skinny youth who again answered the door. His surprised look told me he hadn't expected to see me again.

"Hello again!" I said brightly. "We got off on the wrong foot before, and I think I was misunderstood." Another figure came into view around the door. This guy was burly and mean-looking with a scowl that would have soured milk. He, too, was in his early twenties, but had a shaved head and had a cross in flames tattooed on his neck. He was large, not muscular; although, he would need enormous strength just to be able to lug his bulk around. He was what most people would call obese. It wasn't only his weight that made him repulsive. I had to use all my strength of concentration to not look shocked at his sheer size. He had rolls of fat on his neck, the skin creases yawning open when he moved, revealing the sweat trapped there. The rolls of flabby tissue continued to his wrists, oddly making it look as if he had fleshy sleeves. He appeared decidedly unclean and his clothes had spent their lifetime without seeing a washing machine. His hands were filthy, too; his bitten fingernails looked as if he had been digging in dirt.

I thought I would pre-empt any further hostility by remaining jovial. "Hello," I said breezily, greeting him, too. "I'm looking for someone . . ."

"Never heard of him," Burly interrupted.

"But I haven't described him to you. How would you know if you knew him or not?"

"You told him his name before," said Burly with a slight lisp, indicating Skinny. "I heard it then."

I pressed on, pretending I hadn't heard him. "His name is Kyle. He was at the rave on Spadina last night. I was told he visited here after the rave."

"You heard wrong." The door started to close again.

"My source was very reliable," I continued seriously, with my foot ready to block the threshold. "Is there anyone else here that might remember?"

"Whaddaya mean . . . *source*?" lisped Burly, looking at Skinny, then back at me. "You better come in."

Now we were getting somewhere. I stepped in and closed the door behind me, when it happened once more. There was a sharp pain just above my neck and the floor was again resting by my cheek as I felt myself drift to sleep.

Chapter 11

There have been times in the past when I have woken up in strange places, not knowing where I was or how I got there. Those times are usually associated with my early twenties, opening-night parties or closing-night parties, and way too much booze. The worst was when I was up for a Dora, a Toronto theatrical award. The Dora Mavor Moore Award has been described as the Canadian version of the Tony Awards, except that tickets to the event are cheaper, there is no national TV coverage, and outside the Canadian theatrical circle, most of the nominees are unknown — the curse of anonymity Canadian actors endure. It has often been suggested that Canadian actors are all really members of the witness protection program.

I don't remember much of the rest of the night, the ride home in the cab — I assume it was in a cab — or arriving at home at all. Consequently, I woke up the next morning, fully dressed and prone on the floor, with what I thought to be multiple fatal injuries. My head pounded like a spike had been driven through it, and my body was wracked with horrible joint pain. I couldn't stand. I thought I was dying. I wasn't dying though. It was just the mother of all hangovers.

This was just the way I felt when I awoke from my front-door encounter with the Pack Boys. My head pounded, my stomach felt tight, and my joints ached. I was, in fact, dreaming of that night at the Doras when I regained consciousness. I had yet to determine whether I dreamed it because my head felt like it had been held in a vice, I was nauseous, and I couldn't move to get up. Strangely, the one thing that did occur to me was familiarity: I had experienced this before, so I knew it wasn't fatal; although, in truth, I had never been through anything quite like this. It gradually came to me that I hadn't been drinking, this wasn't that night at the Doras, and I vaguely remembered I was trying to find some kid named Kyle.

I heard voices mumbling not far away. I was face down with my nose and mouth resting against fabric, so I tried to lift my head to see who was talking. I couldn't lift my head though. I could only turn it, and even that was difficult. My eyes opened to find I was facing a wall. The air was damp and mouldy, and I had the impression I might be in the basement of an old house. I heard a shuffling step behind my head. Something was horribly wrong, because when I tried to lift my head to look the other way, my face remained stuck to the fabric. I pulled a little harder and felt a tearing sensation in my cheek, making me cry out at the pain. The pain cleared my head a bit, but a rag in my mouth muffled my yelp.

It came to me that I must have been here for a while. The blood from a gash on my head had run over my face and dried, sticking my cheek to the fabric of my own pants. I realized I was sitting on the floor bent over with my neck duct-taped to my legs and my wrists taped to my ankles, folded over in a permanent toe-touch stretch. I wasn't going anywhere. In a panic, I tried again to wrench my head to look around, painfully pulling my cheek from my pants and causing the tape to tear the hair out of the back of my head, only to see, too late, a kick come crashing into my side. I struggled to get my breath through my nose, as my mouth was full of a filthy rag. I could make out Burly and another who had just delivered the kick. It might have been Skinny, but I couldn't see very well between my eyes watering and the dim light in the small space we occupied.

I glanced around looking for some way out of this mess. I discerned I wasn't in a basement; I was in a small room directly across the hallway from the front door. I could see the front door through a mesh panel, woven like a cane-back chair, in the bottom of the closed door to my prison. In my proximity to the floor I took notice that it was wood and hadn't been cleaned in a very long time. The paint on the wall and door trim were old too, and peeling and flaking in places. Through the mesh, I could see an ugly planter with a tall artificial palm tree beside the front door, on the hinge side. It looked like it had been taken from the entranceway of a pizza joint. On the other side of the door, the latch side, was a large old wooden coat rack. Standing up in the spot intended for umbrellas was a child-sized baseball bat. It was hopeless.

"You shoulda' just walked away," said the kicker in a condescending tone. He kicked me again to drive home his point. Burly grabbed me by the hair, lifting my head, knees and feet a few centimetres off the ground, before swinging my head down sideways, slamming it on the floor. I tried to scream, but I felt the rag start to creep further to the back of my throat, making me feel dangerously close to gagging. My eyes began watering again, as I tried to catch my breath. My head throbbed, and my chest felt like I was being stabbed every time I inhaled. My rib must have been broken from that last kick, I thought. Burly then roughly grabbed my shirt at the shoulders and yanked me upright again, shooting another pain through my chest. I could still faintly smell gas, which reminded me what this was all about. He was right; I should never have come back to the door a second time. I tried to wriggle my hands to see if I could stretch the tape or tear it, but they had wound it too well and too many times. They watched me struggle with the tape, but they weren't worried. They were grinning.

Through the scrim on the bottom of the door I caught some movement out of the corner of my eye. There was a frosted window in the front door, and a shadow of a person started to grow as someone outside clumped up the wooden stairway toward the door. The front door swung open, revealing the darkness outside. It was dark? How long had I been here? A streetlamp in front of the house cast the growing silhouette of this newcomer. He came in and slammed the door, standing there, waiting. I heard a cellphone buzz. The stranger reached into his jacket pocket for the phone and read a message on it, then began to tap out a reply. Burly didn't have the advantage of the see-through panel as I did so he had no idea who was there. He warily opened the door in front of me and the stranger looked at Burly, and then at me on the floor. I watched the stranger for a few moments. He was in his mid-twenties with dark, short gelled hair. He was dressed well, in a brown jacket over a black mock neck shirt, black dress pants, and shined shoes. He wore those long shoes with square toes that were fashionable: shoes I had always felt looked too treacherous to walk in, and somewhat clown-like. This guy, in his mid-twenties, was a poseur and stood as if he thought there was a chance someone might take a picture of him at any minute. Whenever he thought no one was looking, he glanced at himself in the hallway mirror, adjusting his gelled black hair to make sure it looked calculatedly dishevelled. Even though he stood quite a distance away, I could smell that he was wearing too much cologne, too, but not drugstore cologne. He had spent some serious money on it, and wanted everyone to know it. He was dressed to impress, down to his fashionable shoes, and wore a chunky gold watch that he kept fiddling with. He was going out.

"What the fuck have you done?" he asked Burly in a disapproving tone, while shaking his head and looking at me. His phone buzzed again.

"He was snoopin' aroun'," explained Burly. "He asked about that kid, Sal: two times."

"Shut up!" said the stranger looking at Burly but indicating me with his chin. He again began drumming out a reply on his phone. Burly called him Sal! This must be the Sal we were looking for. He shook his head at Burly. "Are ya' fuckin' mental? Just shut up about him." So, they did know something about Kyle. I didn't care about Kyle anymore, though. I just wanted to get out of there. I tried making noises in an effort to get their attention. The only noise I could muster through the rag was a cross between a growl and a bark. I wanted them to take the rag out of my mouth so I could explain. They misinterpreted my growling.

"You shut the fuck up!" said Sal pointing a finger at me. "You're in no position to be angry." Burly rested a foot on my ankle as a threat. I started to make softer noises to let them know they were wrong, but they weren't interested. They were too focused on their own problem: what to do about me. Then they began to talk quite freely in front of me in the most chilling way, deciding what to do with me. Skinny began probing my side with the toe of his shoe to annoy me. He caught my broken rib once and it made me jump.

"Cut it out!" barked Sal to Skinny, who stopped poking me right away. "We'll get rid of him later," said Sal. I didn't like the sound of that. His phone buzzed again. He looked at it and chuckled through his nose. "I love Twitter," he laughed.

Behind him, on the frosted front door window, I noticed more growing silhouettes. The doorbell rang and Sal stiffened, snapped his fingers, and made motions to my captors to close the door to my small room. They stepped over me to get into the room with me and pulled the door closed behind them. With my face still up close to the scrim, I could see quite clearly the silhouettes of two people standing in the doorway waiting for it to open.

Sal opened the door to be greeted by two women holding clipboards. They were in knee-length skirts and matching blazers. On their left lapels, they had laminated badges. They identified themselves as census supervisors. I would never have believed it if I hadn't seen it. They looked serious and efficient-looking and when Sal told them he wasn't interested in the census, the taller of the two women, reminded him that refusing to answer the census was a federal offence punishable by a fine or imprisonment. I recognized that voice! These two imposters would probably have fooled me, too, except that once I heard Amanda's voice, I immediately recognized their credit-card sized "official" badges on their lapels as Actors' Equity Association cards.

The most startling thing wasn't that Amanda was doing all the talking, it was that beside her, made up, dressed in a skirt and high heels, was Bid.

"How many people occupy this dwelling?" asked Amanda as if she were a prosecutor.

"No one," said Sal, sounding bothered.

"When you say 'no one,' do you mean no one besides you?" asked Amanda. What the hell was she doing? *Just call the police* I was willing her. I must have budged, because Burly put a foot on one of my ankles and raked some skin off it with his shoe. Then he warned me to keep still by placing his shoe on top of the abrasion he had just inflicted and increased the pressure, causing searing pain to shoot up my leg.

"Nobody lives here," said Sal. "We're renovating it to rent it out later."

"I see," said Amanda. Bid nodded and marked something on her clipboard. She wasn't wearing her glasses. Amanda was wearing Bid's glasses. Amanda pushed the glasses up to the bridge of her nose. "This is a beautiful old house," continued Amanda, while she leaned her head in, looking around. "Oh, and I love the hardwood floors. They add so much value to a house, and they're so rare in this neighbourhood. These should look beautiful once they're finished . . . and wait a minute — is that a Duncan Phyfe?" she asked breathily, touching the frame of her glasses as if that would better her focus and pointing at the old coat rack that held the baseball bat.

Sal looked over at the rack and stared at it for a few seconds before shrugging. "I have no idea."

"That'll be worth a fortune," she said. Sal must have been convinced, because he stuck out his bottom lip and lifted his eyebrows as he leaned in for a closer look at it. In the meantime, while Sal scrutinized the coat rack, I saw Bid look in the other direction and lob something small into the palm tree planter. She spun back quickly and silently to resume writing on her clipboard without Sal even suspecting anything. What the hell was that all about?

"Well, good luck with the renovations," said Amanda taking one last approving look around. "Good night." And they were off.

Sal closed the door and waited, watching the frosted window on the door until their silhouettes vanished before he said loudly, "Okay, they're gone!" My two guardians slowly swung open the door. It seemed to me that they were afraid the two census women would still hear them. Sal turned to look at them where they stood with their lips tightly clenched. They looked like they were afraid to breathe. Sal looked down at me and then back at the other two. "All right, let's hear it; who is this jamoke?"

"We don't know his name. He came nosing around for that kid, Sal," said Burly. "We told him we never heard of him, but he came back again. So we wrapped him up, like."

Sal ran his hand through his hair and said, "You figured that this was better than just closing the door on him?" He sighed. "You guys are fuckin' morons." Burly started to say something, but Sal held up his hand. "Never mind. I already know what you think." Sal's cellphone rang. He held up one finger while he answered the phone. "Yeah? . . . right . . . okay, I'm coming." He snapped it shut. "I gotta' go, they're opening up and it's late." He shook his head. "Keep this guy here on ice for a while. I'll be back later." Then he waved his finger slowly back and forth between them while saying, "Don't do anything stupid." Then he left. I was hoping that that included not harming me in any way.

They stood there silently for a few seconds after he had gone, just staring at the door, while I lay there folded and taped like an envelope. There was a foul rag stuffed in my mouth, I was sure that I had a broken rib, and I couldn't breathe very well. When they had originally stuffed the rag into my mouth, I must have involuntarily positioned my tongue to refuse its entry, so now my tongue was jammed behind the rag against my soft palate, adding an even bigger impediment to breathing. I tried to relax to use as little air as possible. Shallower breaths also meant my chest wouldn't rise as far, which would, in turn, lessen the pain from my broken rib. It worked for a while, and then I began to feel dizzy.

Chapter 12

I don't know how long I was out, but when I came to in the darkness of that small room, I was alone. The light from the hallway spilled under the door through the mesh panel. My mouth felt like an undertaker's boot. My tongue was swollen and raw, and the back of my neck suffered as if it had a rope burn where the tape was. I was trying to think clearly and not so much about how I got into this mess, but how to get out of it. I couldn't move or communicate. I was feeling hopeless.

"He's on his way!" yelled a squeaky voice coming down the stairs above my head.

"Whafore?" said Burly, his voice muffled. He was walking in from another direction and stood on the other side of the scrim. I watched a few crumbs and a piece of bread land on the floor on the other side of the door from me next to his shoes. He was stuffing his face with a sandwich. "It's too early," he added through a mouthful of food. A cellophane wrapper with a bar code on it dropped to the floor. He didn't bother to pick it up. He just kicked it to the baseboard where some other debris sat.

I couldn't see their faces. The screen on the door only afforded me a view up to their knees. They were standing close and I recognized the pants and the running shoes belonging to Skinny and, of course, the thick ankles beneath the short pants of his pal.

"Well, he's on his way back. He's bringing someone that knows what to do with the guy."

"The kid too?" asked Burly. "Should I bring him down?"

"I dunno," said Skinny. "He didn't say nothin' 'bout the kid. Just leave him up there." So, Kyle was somewhere upstairs. That was something, I guess. But the rest of it wasn't good. They had singled me out for something and they were bringing someone who knew what to do about me.

I heard a car door slam outside, then another. I watched the two growing silhouettes approach the door. The way they had treated me was any evidence of the way they were going to treat me, I was in for a rough ride. The panic rose in my throat as I imagined being taken to Toronto Harbour and dropped off the edge encased in cement. I remembered Dr. Phil saying, "The best predictor of future behaviour is past behaviour." The door opened and Sal entered with another man. I had seen enough gangster movies to know they always brought in an outsider to get rid of a nuisance.

"I'll get the boys to bring him out," he said to the new stranger while closing the front door. Then with a noticeable change in his tone, I heard him say sharply, "Get him."

I watched in horror as Burly and Skinny approached my small room. Skinny opened the door and Burly grabbed me by the heels and rapidly dragged me across the wooden floor. He swung my legs around and dropped them with a clunk so my ankle bones smashed to the floor and I faced Sal. His friend was behind me. Because I was still taped up, my head and hip made contact with the floor almost as abruptly. I had shut my eyes with the pain when the newcomer spoke up.

"Well, well, well," he said with just a hint of an English accent. "It's amazing what lost things will turn up in the back of a closet." He was standing above me now with his hands on his hips. Although his face was obscured by the light fixture directly above him giving his head a corona, I noticed a scar on his neck and the familiar hairline. Of course, the voice was unmistakable. It was Nigel giving the performance of his life, or rather, my life.

He wore a long coat over a suit. He had thrown the sides of the coat open so he could stick his hands into his pants pockets. He nudged my foot playfully with the toe of his shoe, like he was checking to see if I was still alive.

"Yes, this is mine," he said looking down at me with an evil grin and a breathy tone that said he was inconvenienced. "Angelo," he said to me in a most patronizing tone, "you need to be more careful about how you talk to people." Then he turned to Sal and very business-like explained, "As I said, he was supposed to try to find this punk who owes me. I guess he got a bum steer in this direction." Angelo? I was Angelo? What was Nigel up to?

I was lying on the floor, still folded in half, and wondering what could possibly happen next. Nigel was brilliant. I looked back and forth between Nigel and Sal, hoping Sal would buy Nigel's character. I could tell by the way Sal looked at me he wasn't completely sold, but his inexperience and youth were no match for Nigel's expertise and charm.

"Tell me about this punk you're looking for," said Sal, relaxing and ignoring the fact that I was lying on the floor at his feet.

"He's a kid," said Nigel, casually, "about eighteen, a know-it-all and a big-mouth, but he's enterprising, so he was useful to me. His name is Kyle something. He's a freelancer, so he can move on quickly if he wants to. He owes me, and I mean to collect in a hurry, before he disappears. He buys and sells whatever he can get his hands on. Right now it's K."

Skinny and Burly shot a look over at Sal, who glared back at them and shook his head almost imperceptibly. I was bulging my eyes out at Nigel, trying to get his attention. I was damned uncomfortable, too, lying on my side and my left hand was going numb. He noticed me.

"Can we let Angelo get up?" said Nigel pleasantly. "I'm going to need him later."

Sal nodded and motioned to Burly, who grunted and left the room.

"We're going to have to get together in a few days to talk more about an arrangement," continued Nigel again in his matter-of-fact tone, ignoring me. "I'll put together a few numbers and we can try to narrow it down to where we can both meet our objectives with mutual satisfaction."

"I'm sure we'll come to an understanding," said Sal, trying to match Nigel's polished manner by slowing the cadence of his speech and trying to hit all his consonants, revealing that he had accepted Nigel's dominance in the situation. He evidently wanted something from Nigel. Burly came back with a large pair of scissors and bent over me to begin cutting the binding off my neck.

"Please be careful with the tape," said Nigel in a genial tone and smiling. "I want his skin to remain on his neck and face. He's no good to me if he looks like a burn victim."

Burly looked at Nigel as if he didn't understand.

"Just cut it," said Sal a little too sharply, "and let him peel it off himself." Burly nodded, and began to try to cut the tape at the right side of my neck. The cold scissor blade felt dangerous as he struggled with the duct tape that had rolled at the sides, making it difficult to cut. The tape was sticking to the scissors causing the edges to bind to one another. He had to use two hands to pull the handles apart at one point and then see-saw the blades to make any headway. Burly hadn't been this close to me before. He had the blended stench of a little starch, a little fish, and a little bit of old urine. As he toiled at cutting the tape, he huffed and puffed. Even his breath stank: burgers, onions, too much coffee, and a lack of oral hygiene. He reeked of willful social ruin.

"Angelo, I think you owe me a little debt for rescuing you tonight," said Nigel looking down at me. "I think a bottle of something nice."

"What about a bottle of Grey Goose?" said Sal with a chuckle. Then, as if I wasn't still tied up on the floor, he leaned over to me and said jokingly, "I didn't have any tonight, so Robert here had to make do with soda." Nigel gave me a knowing look.

"Good idea!" said Nigel, just as I felt the tape slacken. "Grey Goose it is, Angelo."

Burly was working on the tape around my ankles and wrists now, while Skinny, as if he were picking up a dead fly, used two fingers to take hold of the rag and pull it from my mouth. The rag had been in my mouth so long that it had sucked up all the moisture and was sticking to my tongue and teeth. My jaw was sore from being jammed open, and my mouth felt raw. I was incapable of talking. He threw the rag toward the wall where it fell behind some junk piled up there. I saw Nigel discreetly take a step back, turn quickly, and scoop something out of the planter by the door. He had his hands back in his pockets in a flash and no one but I was the wiser. Nigel stepped forward and helped me to stand up, but my legs were weak. My left arm was starting to tingle as the blood rushed back into it. I tried to say thank you, but my voice was gone. I just rasped and croaked.

"Get him some water," said Sal to Skinny, who ran out of the room.

I nodded to Sal in an attempt to show him some gratitude, but he ignored me. His phone buzzed again and he was preoccupied with the screen.

"Twitter," he said smiling to Nigel. There was bitterness in his smile, but it was clear he thought he was charming and that anything he said was spellbinding. However he got it, Sal appeared to have money and he bought what he considered the outward signs of wealth: clothes, cologne and jewellery. He probably picked clothes by the label, wine by the price, and I would bet he was thinking of taking up golf so he could carry expensive clubs in the trunk of his car. He was under the delusion that money made him powerful. Sure, it gave him a type of power with people like Skinny, Burly, and the people who worked at the rave. Right now, he did have power over me, and I am sure he thought he had a peer relationship with Nigel's character; although, that was a total fantasy.

"I'll call you in a few days to make arrangements to meet again," said Nigel, briefly holding up a business card which I presumed was Sal's and then popping it into his breast pocket. He reached into his inside jacket pocket and gave Sal a business card of his own. I tried not to look shocked. I was concentrating on remaining upright on my wobbly legs while carefully peeling the tape off without removing a layer of skin. Skinny arrived back in the hallway with a small bottle of water, which he passed to me along with his trademark tart look. I nodded thanks to Skinny.

"You need a ride somewhere?" asked Sal while I drained the bottle. "I'll have one of the boys take you in the Bimmer."

"Thanks, but no," said Nigel laughing. I handed the empty water bottle and the tape back to Skinny who just threw it down on the floor, while his eyes never left me. "I think Angelo will want to stretch his legs a bit." Burly looked like he didn't understand and

Skinny gave his trademark lemon-pucker smile. Sal reached into his pocket, pulled out some keys, and said to the boys, "Empty the trunk and don't scratch the car." He pushed a button on the key fob, which made the car outside chirp, and I saw the glow of flashing headlights in the frosted window on the door. Then he threw the keys to Skinny. Nigel and Sal shook hands and Sal's phone buzzed again. We left while he replied to another tweet on his phone.

We had just reached the sidewalk on Baldwin when we heard the door click shut behind us and the trunk of the black BMW open. Nigel walked casually with his hands still in his pockets, making a show of looking at the quaint houses on either side as if admiring the neighbourhood. "Just keep walking casually," he said hissing through clenched teeth and smiling. "I'm sure we are being watched." We had reached the end of the block and I had a quick look back as we rounded the corner. The boys were carrying boxes into the house, and they were running with them. As we turned the corner my legs felt a bit better and Nigel finally spoke, but in a hushed tone.

"Holy shit!" he hissed. "You can't even imagine the night I've had."

Chapter 13

We hailed a cab on Spadina. As soon as we were in, I turned around to see if we were being followed, but there was so much traffic as we headed north that I could not tell. I had to turn back again and face the front. The pain in my chest was too much. "Let's go to Bloor and get on the subway. It'll be harder to track us," I croaked at Nigel. "And call Amanda. Tell her to phone the police."

"Right," Nigel said quietly. He leaned forward and said to the driver, "Bloor and Spadina." Then he phoned Amanda. "She's not answering," he said. He left her a voice mail telling her to contact the police.

I sat back in the rear seat and watched the driver's eyes alternate between the traffic on the road ahead and us in the back seat. He looked nervous, like he was trying to memorize our faces in case we appeared later on the news. We must have looked desperate.

We took the subway for one stop, switched trains to double back, and got off at Bathurst station. We took the back way out of the station at Markham Street. It was a little darker at that exit, there were fewer people, and it would be easier to fade into the background, or see if someone were coming at us. We walked in the shadows of the tree-lined street for the last few blocks to my apartment building. My

101

legs had started to feel better, except for my ankles where they had been slammed to the floor, and the ankle scrapes from Burly's shoes. My head ached and my rib smarted when I breathed too deeply. We didn't speak on the way to my place. I was still pondering how narrowly I had escaped, and I was worried I was only dreaming my rescue.

"You really look like shit, you know," bellowed Nigel from the living room, in what I'm sure he thought was a conciliatory tone. I was alone in my bedroom, standing in nothing but my underwear, in front of a full-length mirror. He had a point. Although I had wiped most of the blood off my face, I looked like someone who had come in last place in a barroom brawl. The hair on the side and back of my head was matted with dried blood, a spot the size of a softball on one side of my chest was starting to turn blue, and my ankles were raw and bruised. My lower back was starting to ache, too, from being bent over for so many hours, but I felt elated. There is nothing like a narrow escape to make you feel invulnerable. I walked into the bathroom and threw up. There was nothing in my stomach so it was painfully wrenching and my rib complained angrily.

"I'm going to take a shower," I yelled to Nigel in the other room. "I won't be long. Then I want to hear everything."

I felt safe in the shower, surrounded by all that was familiar. It was small and warm and comforting, except where the hot water stung my ankle. The stinging reminded me that I hadn't dreamed this. I lowered my head under the stream of warm water and watched the runoff turn pink and then red and then back to pink again as the blood washed out of my hair and swirled into the drain. Once it ran clear, I knew it was time to get out.

Nigel was sitting on the couch staring straight ahead as I walked in dressed in fresh clothes and gently patting my hair dry with a towel. I was still leaving the occasional pink bloodstain on the white towel. He stood up when he saw me and handed me an empty glass into which he poured a liberal amount of my Scotch.

"Sit," he said. I didn't need to think about it twice. I collapsed into the couch and winced at the shooting pain in my side. "What the hell went on in there?" He continued. "You were wrapped up like — well, I've never seen anything like that before. What happened?"

"I'll need a few minutes to wrap my head around it," I said, still feeling confused. "I'll get to it, but first," I took a large gulp of the Scotch. "They were carrying boxes into the house," I said, referring to the packages Skinny and Burly were moving between the car and the house. "I wonder what was in those?"

"Dope, I'll bet," said Nigel. "These guys are a small group, but they are into a number of things. Drugs are the main focus right now. It sounds like they hijacked a truck about two years ago. From what Sal told me, companies frequently use trucks with company logos that don't match what's inside as a disguise. The truck they grabbed had a plant care company logo on the side. I think they could not believe their luck. They were aiming for electronics, but the truck was full of pharmaceuticals. They put the dope into storage, and they draw some of it out when they need to replenish their stock at the house. They use the rave and other places to move the stock. Sal called it his distribution channel. This Sal is not too bright, either. He just got lucky. He is only in charge because of the calibre of the chuckleheads who work for him and the fact that he has his money.

"He started out with an agreement to sell the dope at a rave about a year and a half ago. There was another guy that had an agreement at the time, but Sal had undercut the other guy's prices, and he gave the rave owner a bigger cut of the profits. So, the other guy was let go. A lot of money must have changed hands, too, because the owner of the

103

rave sold it to Sal a few months ago. Apparently raves change hands all the time. Anyway, Sal thought this was a good idea, because he could increase his profit margin on the dope, which is where the real money is, and cover the costs of the rave with the revenue from the booze and cover charges. The drugs are his main enterprise but I think that owning the place makes him feel like a big shot, and that is the most important thing to him."

"How do you know all this?"

"As I said, he's not too bright. It seems more important to him that people think he is a big wheeler and dealer. He told me most of what I am telling you. The rest I gleaned from what wasn't said, and from others who wandered up while he was talking to me. Occasionally, he would have to go off to take care of something. Whoever had come in at the tail end of the conversation thought I was on the inner circle so they kept talking as if I were in the know. We also made a quick stop on the way over here at a self-storage place around Cherry Street and Lakeshore, where he put a few boxes into the car. I didn't go in with him, though. He asked me to stay in the car. I sat there for a few minutes, staring at rows of green garage doors."

"I guess that's where they store the dope. What the hell have we gotten into?" I said. "This is it, though. I'm out. Those guys are crazy. I think they were starting to make plans to get rid of me. Did you know that Amanda and Bid showed up? Bid, for God's sake! You should have seen them; they were doing a survey! Who the hell dragged Bid into this mess?"

"You saw them?" asked Nigel incredulously. "They didn't see you."

"There was a small scrim I could see through in the door of the room where they kept me. I thought those guys were going to kill me! When you first arrived I thought you were their finger man." My adrenaline was kicking in again, making me ramble and jump from topic to topic. "This kid, Kyle — he has no idea what he's into. Well, maybe he does, at that; I think he's in a room upstairs in that house. They made reference to bringing him down." Then, what Nigel had said a few seconds before struck me and I jumped back a few thoughts. "You knew that Amanda and Bid were there, too?"

"Yeah, Amanda called to let me know you had gone into the house for the second time and hadn't come out after an hour," said Nigel. "She said they had dumped you in an alley and sprayed you with gasoline the first time. What was that all about, and why the hell did you go in again?"

"Stupidity," I said, weakly. "Okay, wait . . . I have a few questions. . ." The door buzzed.

"That's Amanda," said Nigel walking to the door and pushing the button to let her in. "Hold that thought. Before you ask, I called her while you were in the shower. We might as well have all the players put all the pieces together."

I was standing up at the counter putting another Scotch into my glass when Amanda, Bid, and Karen walked in looking worried; Nigel had cautioned Amanda on the phone that I was in rough shape. Amanda and Nigel grilled me with questions and I wasn't long bringing everyone up to speed as to what had happened to me while I was in the care of those hoods. But, I had questions of my own.

"What possessed you to masquerade as census takers?" I asked Amanda. "And what were you trying to accomplish?"

"We needed to see if you were all right," said Amanda. "First, I tried looking around where you were dumped in the alley, but you weren't there. I even poked around the old tires. So, I figured you were still inside the house."

"Why didn't you just knock on the door? Why the disguise?"

"Well, we needed a Plan B. If you weren't in plain sight, we needed another way to get intelligence," she said. "That's where Bid came in. I called her to ask for advice."

"I wasn't doing anything anyway," said Bid with a shrug, "and I figured you could use some technical help." She had her glasses back on and had changed into her usual clothes.

"Bid's plan was to plant a bug in the house to see if they would talk about you once we were gone," said Amanda.

"You planted a bug? Where would you get a bug?" I asked Bid.

"Oh, right," said Nigel suddenly. He reached into his right-hand coat pocket and handed something small to Bid. "This would be yours."

"You have to be imaginative," said Bid smiling and holding it up. It was her cellphone wireless headset. "Just about everybody has a bug these days. I placed a phone call to Amanda's cellphone from mine just before we went in the front door. Once we were inside, when I had the chance I tossed my Bluetooth headset into the potted plant. The headset acted like a remote microphone. Once we left, all we had to do was listen to Amanda's phone to hear what was going on. We had to stick close, though. We only had about a ten-metre range between my phone and the headset before it lost the signal." She popped it into a side pocket of the big bag she always carried.

"Over the headset, we heard them talking about you. We found out that they didn't know your name," said Amanda. "We also heard them call one of the guys Sal, who took a phone call and had to leave. I assumed it was the Sal we'd heard about earlier. We watched him leave while we hid behind a parked car outside and then we phoned Nigel to let him know what we had found out, and of course, to give him Sal's description."

"I was already at the rave when I got the call," Nigel jumped in, "and when Sal walked in a few minutes later matching their description, I decided to kill two birds with one stone. I was going to try to make contact with him, but he beat me to it. I was just standing there with a soda water and he introduced himself to me. He'd been notified ahead, I guess, that I was a person of interest. He even knew I had ordered a Grey Goose but had to settle for soda. That embarrassed him a bit, I think. I was easy for him to pick out too. I was way overdressed for that place.

"Although the place is a rave, he treats it like it's legit. He questioned why I was there because he had never seen me before. He is obviously, and thankfully, not a theatre patron," he said as an aside. "I let him know I was looking for a kid that had pissed me off and owed me money. I told him I had heard Kyle was there the night before. Then for some reason I can't imagine, he assumed that I wanted to buy the place, so I just played along. From Amanda's call, I knew you were a prisoner, too, so I let him know I had sent you to visit his place to get information on the kid. Of course I didn't tell him I knew you were still there. He suggested we take a ride and in the car, that he thought you might be still there, and he mentioned there might have been a misunderstanding. He does have an annoying habit of constantly checking his cellphone. He told me that he has just discovered Twitter. It's a miracle we didn't hit anything as he was reading and texting while driving. Not only that, he's doing something he called geotagging, which he says he has automatically switched on, whatever that means. The rest you know."

"You wore your Actors' Equity cards on your lapels!" I said turning to Bid. "What if he'd read them? Didn't you worry about the risk?"

"Ah, you know they're Equity cards," said Bid with her index finger up, "but, he's never seen them before. You also probably didn't notice that the left-hand corner of each card was tucked under our lapels. In fact, it was gaffer-taped there so they wouldn't move. All he would have seen is the word *Canadian* on a card plastered with the Canadian flag. It was too dark in there anyway to read the small print on the cards. Amanda's plan was to keep talking and to escalate the volume or just leave if he got suspicious."

Karen had been silent the whole time, listening with a look of disbelief on her face. She slowly walked over to me and with tears in her eyes hugged me. The pain was unbearable and I cried out, which made her jump back.

"Sorry," I said. "I'm just a bit sore."

"My God! What happened?" she asked. "I had no idea that things were going to turn out this way." She began to cry silently.

"I just took a few kicks in the side to keep me quiet." I tried to make it sound trivial.

"Let's have a look," said Bid heading over. "Get that shirt off."

"What?"

"Come on, come on! Don't make me ask you again."

I started to undo the buttons and swung one side of the shirt back, which was painful. I must have made a face because Bid said, "Okay, stop. I'll help. Don't worry, I'll be gentle." She carefully opened the shirt and said nothing. She just inspected me, stone-faced. Amanda looked over, and her face stiffened. Karen threw her hands up to her mouth. What were they looking at? It was just a small bruise. It didn't look so bad in the mirror before I took a shower.

I glanced down and saw a transformation had occurred. One side of my chest was black and blue.

"That hot shower you took made the bruising come up quicker," said Bid as she hurried away from me. She went to her bag, fished out a wide-roll bandage and returned promptly to me. "That needs to be bound and immobilized, and you need a doctor." She started to roll the long bandage around my chest deftly and firmly, but without hurting me, while I held my arms out.

"You keep bandages in your bag?" I was flabbergasted. "What *don't* you keep in there?"

She ignored my question while she finished binding my chest. "Okay, now, let's have a look at that head," she said as she stepped behind me and eased me onto a chair. She took a pen from my counter and I felt her gently lift my hair with it and lightly touch my head with her fingertip. "You have a couple of good-sized goose eggs there. There's a small gash, too, but it's relatively minor. It's stopped bleeding," she paused, "but it's still open. Let's see what we can do about that."

"Only a small cut? There was a hell of a lot of blood," said Nigel. "It was caked on him when I first saw him."

"A small laceration on the head can seem a lot worse than it really is," said Bid, heading back to her bag. "Nothing bleeds like the head." She must have seen my puzzled look because she added, "I'm the health and safety officer of the theatre. Let's get some ice on that head." She was pointing at Karen. Karen went to the fridge while Bid snapped on some purple gloves.

"The health and safety officer knows where to find the first aid kit. You used the word *laceration*," I said, "and what's with those gloves? Do you work in a back room at the border?"

"Three years as a Canadian Forces medic," she confessed deadpan, coming back to me with a small tube in her hand.

"We're learning much today," said Nigel.

"Antiseptic?" I asked, meaning the tube in her hand. "Will this hurt?"

"Not just antiseptic, liquid sutures, too," she said going around the back of me aiming for my head wound. "It may smart a bit. Be a big boy. Be brave." She was right; it stung. "You still need a doctor. Now, don't move your head for a few seconds while I hold the wound closed until it binds."

I remembered something. "Nigel," I tried not to move my head. "I saw you hand Sal a business card. What was that?"

"That was a souvenir prop from a film I did a few years ago," he said. I thought I might need something to legitimize my character, so I brought it." He shrugged. "Robert was the name on the card, so I used that name."

"What about the contact info on the card?" asked Amanda.

"New York," smiled Nigel. "I think that impressed Sal, too. I hope he doesn't phone the number. It's a pizza place in Brooklyn."

"Okay," said Bid behind me, patting my shoulder. "Your head's closed up."

"Well, this was all very exciting, and most of us came away unscathed, but it's time the police were involved," I offered. "They're not going to like that we were playing amateur sleuths, and I suspect we will get yelled at. But now it's time to hang up our magnifying glasses and deerstalkers. Karen, you'll have to go to the police." Karen conspicuously said nothing, and both she and Amanda had guilty looks on their faces. "Karen? The police?"

"I can't," she said, hanging her head.

"She can't," said Amanda looking at each of us.

Chapter 14

I didn't think the day could have turned any stranger. It had started with a jolt out of bed, and escalated from there. I think it was Samuel Goldwyn who said, "Start out with an earthquake and work up to a climax." Well, I had made good on that piece of cinematic advice today, but it was time for the finale, I thought. Unfortunately, once again, I was out-voted by the circumstances.

"Everybody, sit down," announced Bid as she strode into the room with a stack of glasses tucked carefully under her crooked arm, a jug of water, and my bottle of Scotch. "I have an uneasy feeling about this."

Karen's face looked as if she had seen someone killed, but with each breath, she appeared to be gathering her strength. The room was silent except for the sound of Bid pouring Scotch and water into the glasses. When the last glass was poured, Karen took a breath and said, "It's Rob." She paused so long, that I thought I would help with some background.

"Rob is her husband and Kyle's father," I offered the rest of the group. "Right now he's in Ottawa on some kind of business." Then to Karen, I said, "What about Rob?"

"While we were driving back to Toronto last night, he got a call from Ottawa." she began. "There is an emergency meeting there. He had to fly back there on the first flight this morning."

"Have you told your husband what's going on since this morning?" asked Bid.

"There is no phone contact," Amanda replied. "He's in seclusion."

"What kind of seclusion?" Nigel asked suspiciously. "What's going on?"

"The phones are all surrendered before they go into these meetings," she replied.

"Rob is a Member of Parliament," interrupted Amanda.

"He's an MP?" I said, surprised. This was news to me. "Wait a minute — what's his name?"

"Rob Eaton," said Karen, as if I should have already known it.

"Robert Eaton?" said Nigel throwing up his hands. "He's a Conservative. No wonder Kyle is rebelling. Why are they in seclusion?"

"I can't say," said Karen. "It's confidential party business. They don't tell anyone."

Nigel threw his hands up again.

"Great!" said Bid, taking charge. "All right, we've established that Rob will be no help to us here. But why can't you go to the police?"

"If we involve the police, they will want to know the whole story," said Karen and then she paused.

"What are you not telling us?" Bid looked serious and Karen blanched. Bid stood up. "Look, Karen, these three have stuck their necks out for you and your wayward kid today. This one," she indicated me with a stabbing motion of her finger, "should be in a cab on the way to the Emerg, so let's have it all, or I'm on the phone now." Karen didn't say a word, so Bid pulled her phone out and held it up, flat in her palm.

"Okay!" Karen shouted. She was clearly angry and nervous, having been backed into a corner. Bid had evidently pushed the right button. "There's not really anything more, it's just the circumstances that present themselves once we go to the police. . . . Kyle has been in trouble before, for various things. They have been petty — mostly — but serious enough to involve the police. He was picked up for driving our car without a licence once; that's how we found out he was borrowing the car at night. We got a call from the police in the middle of the night. He was in an accident once, too. He wasn't driving that time, but they found some drugs on him. He was a minor and there was only a small quantity so they called us into the police station and we brought him home. The police said they thought he was selling the drugs, but they didn't have any proof so they had to let him go for that one, although he was charged with possession. He had to show up in Juvenile Court a few times, and he had to go to counselling. He quit the counselling, even though it was court ordered. He has to go back to court for that in October.

"Last summer, we found drugs in the house, too, baggies of pills. Anyway, he had no explanation, and he showed no remorse. He didn't even seem to care that this was much more serious than his own neck on the line. It was as if he thought we would just leave him alone. If he is picked up again for drugs, it will destroy our family."

"It seems the fabric of your family is already stretched to breaking," said Nigel. "Maybe getting caught and charged will force him to turn around. It sounds to me like he needs a bit of a shake-up from a heavy hand, don't you think?"

"It's not just about him though!" cried Karen. "If he is arrested, they will search our house. If they find drugs, even if we don't know about them, the law says we are responsible and culpable. If they determine that he is selling dope, they can legally seize our house, our car, and any of our possessions if they can even remotely link them to the sale of drugs. Even if they don't find any drugs in our house, the place will be destroyed. Have you any idea how they conduct a search? They rip walls and furniture apart. And, right now, I can't be sure there are no drugs somewhere in the house. But they will determine that he's selling, because he is . . . you told me that."

"But his life may be in danger," said Amanda. "You're only talking about material possessions. There is only an outside chance there are drugs in the house, and there is no guarantee that the police will search your house before you can get to it and search it yourself. You could always rebuild later, if it came to that." She put her arm around Karen.

"It would be impossible to rebuild," said Karen quietly. "If we are held responsible for Kyle's crimes, we will be charged. Even if we aren't put in jail, once the media gets their teeth into us, Rob's political career will be ruined. It's a miracle the media haven't already gotten hold of it and blown it up. You know how they are. They'll seize it and milk the story until we lose everything . . . everything. I can't go to the police. Our reputations will be ruined and we will never be able to work again. Rob's life will be over." She was crying in earnest by now.

The room was silent except for Karen trying to suppress her sobs.

It was time for me to speak up. My instincts as an actor and improviser kicked in. From what we had just heard, we had to try to create a solution on our own. "Right! Well, we can always go to the police later. Let's see what we know and what we can do. What are the options? Nigel, what have we got?"

Nigel jumped in as if we had been sharing the same thought. "First, of course, we have to get Kyle out of that place on Baldwin. We are pretty sure he is on the second floor, because they mentioned him when Michael was there," he said turning to look at everyone as he spoke. I nodded. "We don't know if he is injured, and we don't know if he is tied up, but from their history, I think we can say probably yes to both."

"We can't storm the place," Amanda said. "We don't have the manpower and we don't want to risk any more injuries, or worse. And I am pretty sure from what we've seen these guys are capable of worse."

"We'll have to get them to hand Kyle over voluntarily," I said, thinking out loud. "We'll have to use their weaknesses against them. Like they do in judo or wrestling."

"You're going to threaten them?" asked Karen.

"No, we're going to do what we do best," I said, getting a flash of downright genius. "We are going to trick, distract, and deceive. We don't have much time, though. We only have a small window where the impressions they have of us are still fresh. We only have today to do this." I looked at the clock on the wall. It was three o'clock in the morning. "Today, in fact, has turned into tomorrow, but you know what I mean." I looked around the room. No one was protesting. In fact they all seemed to be waiting to hear the next move. "So, what do you think?"

Bid was the first to speak. "Okay, I think I can see where this is going," she said warily. "I don't like it, but I'm in, on the condition that if this goes south, we call the cops. I'm going to be the voice of sanity in this group, and I'll have the cops on speed-dial."

"I plan to call the cops anyway," I said. "We're going to need them to mop up after we're gone." Everyone turned to face me with bewildered looks.

As plans go, this one didn't start out terribly complicated, but the further we delved into mapping it out, the more creative we got and the more complex it became.

We were tired, I was hurt, and desperate, and we knew we were going to be dealing with criminals who had no scruples and seemed to be too stupid to know when to stop anyway. These thugs sold drugs and kicked people tied up on the floor. We were going to try to deceive them and lull them into a situation where they would suspend their disbelief, as we say in the theatre. We would treat our plan as a show, but there was never a show mounted so quickly or where a bad review could result in calamity.

"Karen, I'm afraid I am going have to ask you to do something rather distasteful, but it's something I need," I began. She started to look uneasy, so I continued hastily, "No, no, don't let your imagination get away from you. It's just that when I see these guys again I want to be wearing the same clothes I wore when we met the first time. Unfortunately those clothes are dirty and spattered with blood. I need them to be clean so there is no evidence they mistreated me. If I look like they've beaten me up, they may feel inclined to do it again; I want to discourage that impulse. There is an all-night laundromat just a few blocks from here, on Bloor at Markham. Could you wash them for me? I know it's a crappy job, but I wouldn't ask if it wasn't important."

"Sure," she said looking somewhat relieved. "What are the plans, though?"

"Truly, I'm not sure yet." I said. "But, I have a few ideas and these three are the smartest people I know. We'll come up with something."

I threw my clothes into a laundry bag and handed it to her. "Please hurry, and by the time you get back, we should have it all figured out." She left under a full head of steam.

"First things first," I said picking up the Scotch bottle and the jug of water. "Let's get rid of the booze. We're going to need clear heads for this." I put on a pot of coffee.

My skeleton of a plan had three elements: we needed to get Kyle to safety; we would plant some kind of incriminating evidence on the premises; and then we'd call the police to arrest these criminals while we escaped. I also liked the idea of getting revenge on the ones who beat me up, but I didn't mind doing it anonymously. I certainly didn't want these guys looking for us later to settle the score. Bid, Nigel, and Amanda agreed to my outline. The trick would be to get it all done and prevent the bad guys from suspecting that we'd played any part in their arrest.

"The only thing that will convince them, though," I said, "is if we appear much more powerful than they are, and we can intimidate them with the size of our organization. It would be best if we could do this without Sal being there. It would be easier to fool Skinny and Burly."

"Who?" asked Amanda.

"Skinny and Burly: the two intellectuals Sal has working for him. You didn't see them. They were in the closet with me when you arrived at the front door."

"That may be something to keep in mind," snapped Nigel. "They've never seen Amanda or Bid. That may come in handy."

"Right," I agreed. "They know Sal has made some kind of business deal, or is about to make a deal with you, Nigel, or rather, Robert. Let's take it for granted that Sal has told them. If he hasn't, fine, but if he has, then it will reinforce what they already know. Even one nugget of truth may make whatever we tell them easier to swallow."

"What are we going to tell them?" asked Nigel.

"We're going to tell them we want Kyle: plain and simple," I said. "We're going to convince them that Sal has told us to get the kid off their hands. Then we're going to create a diversion to make them eager for us to take the kid."

Chapter 15

I have to say that my colleagues were good sports about the whole thing. They worked in a business where they were stressed every day, and their ability to overcome that stress was what their success and livelihood depended upon. There was no question of ever walking away from a difficult situation when they were at work. Theatre people almost never shrink from a challenge. Whether people choose a career in the theatre because they are creative, or they develop creativity because their occupation demands it, is a debate for psychologists and philosophers. The fact is, whatever the reason, theatre people always find a solution to any challenge. Not because they are any braver or smarter than the rest of the population, but because if they don't work, they won't eat. And if you've ever seen an actor eat, you will understand how food motivated we are.

Maybe it was because of those years of conditioning to always find a solution that I was able to convince them to accept my plan to just walk in and ask for Kyle. Maybe they were too fatigued to even balk at my idea. But they didn't just accept the plan; they embraced it as inevitable, and with enthusiasm. They jumped in, offering their opinions and helping to sculpt what we came to believe was the perfect plan.

"Here's what I think will work," began Nigel. "We, Michael and I, walk into the house on Baldwin and boldly tell the guys there that Sal has told us to pick the kid up. We'll insinuate it is a part of an agreement that Sal and I have cooked up over breakfast.

"As I see it, there are three ways this can go, and we have to be prepared for all three. The first is unlikely but most desirable — they just hand the kid over. I don't think that's liable to happen, but I'm hopeful. The next is they just refuse, and the third is that they'll want to call Sal. That is something we cannot let them do."

"You'll have to convince them somehow," said Amanda. "Don't even let them think they have the option of refusing. Maybe you can indicate that you expect Sal has already called them."

"And if they insist on calling Sal? What then?" Bid threw in while bringing me a glass of water and a bottle of Advil.

"*Deus ex machina*," I said. "We need a diversion to change their priorities. Something big enough that will impact on their most basic need: survival.

"Bid, here's where we need your expertise," I said. "We'll need some gunshot squibs: body packs and wall loads — the wireless ones."

"How many?" she asked without hesitation. Then she held up a hand. "Never mind, I'll get all we have. We'll see what we need later. I'll get blood packs too. What else?"

"Props . . . maybe retractable knives, and a breakaway bottle or two?"

"Check," she said. "You need guns? I have some really nice-looking prop guns: Brownings, Berettas, Glocks, and I have a Heckler."

"No! I don't want to provoke them to start peppering us if they have guns, too," I said. "I think I want it to look like someone else is after us. We'll try to make them want to escape the crossfire. Do you have a portable, high-powered spotlight, something hand-held?"

"Right," she said making notes.

"Then, we'll need something that will entice the cops to go into the house once we're finished there," I said.

"Dope!" said Nigel excitedly. "If the cops already know about these guys and are looking for a reason to go in, we would be giving them a perfect opportunity. And if the cops aren't after them, drugs would be a great way to start the heat on them. Can we get dope?" he asked Bid.

"Of course," she said rolling her eyes.

"Not real dope," I said quickly.

"I'm not an actor," she said, "of course, not real dope. I have a case of empty capsules."

"How many in a case?" I asked.

"Sixty thousand," she said, deadpan.

"It sounds like we'll need a van."

"I'm way ahead of you," she said, pulling out her phone.

"Who are you calling at this hour?" I asked.

"Texting," she said. "Tamara can help us with some of this. The squibs and blood are costume department things. I have a feeling we'll need more, too, so the sooner we can get her started, the better."

"What are you going say this is about?" I asked.

"One thing at a time," she said tapping away on the phone with her thumbs.

We understood that the plan's keystone was to make sure Sal wouldn't be at the house on Baldwin. We planned to arrive early in the morning, in only a few hours, so hopefully he would still be at the rave organizing the end of-the-week cleanup or he might be out for breakfast. An early arrival would mean that the two or three people at the house would be disoriented, too. We could take a drive by to see if his BMW was parked out front, but that would take too much time. We needed something else. Then it occurred to me.

"Nigel," I spun around and headed over to my laptop. "Did you say that Sal talked to you about geotagging and Twitter?"

"Yeah, he said he'd just discovered them. He said he couldn't get enough of it, and bent my ear for most of the time I was with him. He seemed to think it would impress me. He used the phrase, *addicted to it*. What's that got to do with anything?"

"If he is new to it, like any newbie, he'll use it all the time. That may be good for us."

"You better let me know what's going on," said Amanda. "Did I miss something?"

"Geotagging is . . ." I was searching for an easy description, while I typed on the laptop. "It's like a treasure hunt . . . sort of . . . only you use your cellphone." I was finding it difficult to describe it while I was distracted with typing out search terms on the computer.

Bid put her phone back on her hip and jumped in. "Geotagging is sort of like using your phone as a mini GPS device. It began by adding precise position information to photographs or websites to give exact location relevance to the data." Everyone turned to look at her like she was an alien. "Like if you want to put photographs onto search engine map software," she continued, looking annoyed, "some high-end cameras come with GPS chips and software that allow photographers to manage their photos by classifying them according to the location where they were taken. They electronically tag the pictures with the longitude and latitude from the global positioning satellites."

"Wow, I didn't know all that," I said. "What I am talking about, though, are the GPS-enabled cellphones. You know how cellphones now have GPS chips embedded in them so that 911 operators can pinpoint their exact location in an emergency?"

"I didn't know even that, but okay, go on," said Nigel. Amanda shrugged, too.

"Well, these phones can also send the location info to the owner's Twitter page or Facebook page to announce to their friends where they are," Bid interjected. "But, it doesn't just come up with a longitude and latitude. People have substituted these numbers with the names of landmarks like the CN Tower, Empire State Building, museums, restaurants, Starbucks, Tim's, street intersections, and even people's apartments. I saw one reference as 'Mom's.' You can do it anywhere, whether you are in New York, Toronto, or Tokyo. It has quickly evolved into a sort of treasure hunt where you can check in at geotagging sites to collect points and pick up virtual or real prizes and coupons from stores and restaurants. The tech savvy marketers now use it as a marketing tool."

"The important thing here, though," I interrupted, "is that Sal has set his phone to automatically check in wherever he is. If his phone is on, he is already telling us where he is every time he passes one of these tagged landmarks. All we have to do . . ."

"Is find his Twitter page to see where he is," Amanda cut in, catching on.

I was already scanning the document where I had pasted the URLs earlier, looking for a reference to Sal or Baldwin or the Pack Boys, anything that would identify him. I hoped to find a link to his Twitter account or his Facebook profile. I looked at the same pages as before, only this time I looked for Sal. The path changed soon after I was down the social networking rabbit hole. Sal was in a few pictures, though there were no tags identifying him. Then we got a break: a photo of him *Pal Sal*. I followed the trail to a collection of hundreds of pictures. It took some time to work our way through them but we found one in a collection owned by a girl named Pooch. She identified him as Sal Bodinov. Bingo! A Facebook page in his name was a dead end.

Undaunted, I looked for Pooch. I couldn't find much that was relevant on her Facebook page, but I got a hit on Twitter. It took some time crawling through her list of over two hundred followers, but we found Sal's Twitter page. It was almost as good as finding him in the flesh because the content was current. He had fresh tweets for the past hour, mostly outgoing. It was like being a fly on the wall, as they say. He was illuminating the world with his thoughts, but it was as dim as the light from a twelve-watt bulb. He was unaware of the permanent nature of his digital vapourings. His tweets confirmed he was still at the rave. He was commenting on the women around him and how, on a dare from one of his cronies, he was going to bed one chosen at random. He was musing on what kind of gymnastics she might be capable of.

Technology natives like Sal, who were born after the invention of the CD and who communicate primarily by text and email, don't have the luxury of pretending that they didn't say what they actually said. It is written in stone — no, it is written electronically, something much more durable than stone. It will be seen by those to whom you sent it, and it may be broadcast to the group that you choose. It will also be copied and sent to those you know nothing about, where it could be forwarded on again, edited and quoted out of context. Then it will be backed up without your knowledge, where it will live forever, because nothing is deleted anymore. Because I'm aware of this, I am very careful of what I say and how I say things in a text or an email. I'm no criminal, but I make my living using language as a craft and as an art form and I am fully aware of its power and of its pitfalls. I know that what I say, or portions of what I say, can be used against me. So, I am careful. Sal was not so careful. I was feeling a bit sorry for the woman whom he had marked as the victim of his sexual sniping. His plan was to use his charisma and her naïveté and conceit to ensnare her in what he thought was his charming trap. So, it was only fitting, I thought, that we, too, were hoping to use his own narcissism to help him drown himself.

As I quickly scanned Sal's tweets, Amanda watched over my shoulder, Nigel poured everyone coffee, and Bid read her phone, which had just beeped.

"Tamara's up and working on the stuff we need," she said. "And she has a minivan: perfect! I told her we would fill her in when she got here," she added.

The door buzzed. "That was fast," said Nigel. He went over to the door with the coffee pot in hand to buzz her in.

"That cannot be Tamara," said Bid. "She hasn't left home yet."

Nigel opened the door to see who it was before they had a chance to knock. It was Karen. We all seemed to have forgotten about her. She walked in carrying my clothes neatly Cellophane-covered on hangers.

"You had them dry cleaned?" I asked.

"The pants were dry cleaned, the shirt was laundered," said Karen. "I was going to throw them into the washer, but the woman who worked behind the counter said she was just about to start a cleaning cycle. She said it would take about a half-hour less to do it that way, so I said sure."

"How is everything going?" she asked tentatively. She looked tired. I looked around the room. Everyone looked tired. This had been a long day, and it was nowhere near over. I draped the cleaning over the back of a chair. Nigel brought Karen some coffee and filled her in on what we had so far. I went back to the laptop. He let her know that we had ordered some props and other equipment and that was where he stopped dead. When I looked up from the laptop, they were both staring at me expectantly.

"Karen," I began, not knowing where I was going, "it may sound crazy at times, but stay with us. We're going to get Kyle, and we're going to get him this morning."

"Okay," was all she said. She started to smile, but then looked like she figured there were conditions to the rescue. She was right. She was looking at me, anticipating more information, but I had nothing further to give her yet. If I told her everything we had discussed up to now, she would think we were barking mad.

Chapter 16

At 3:10 a.m., the door opened and Tamara walked in dragging a small, two-wheeled luggage cart behind her. Over her shoulder, she had a strap that held up a red metal tool case with a lock on the front. There was an identical one on the luggage cart, as well as a black soft-sided bag. "Take this, will ya," she said to Nigel, indicating the case that hung over her shoulder. He took the strap and almost toppled over when he lifted it off her shoulder.

"Jesus, what's in this? Gold bars?" he groaned.

"Detonators," she said. "Actors," she muttered and shook her head. "All flash and no substance." She was teasing him about the weight of the box.

"Well — it took me by surprise," whined Nigel. "I was off balance. If I had known . . ." he trailed off as he placed it on the floor with a clunk.

"Careful with that," snapped Tamara as she negotiated the cart through the door. "My God, is there coffee? I'll be cranky without coffee."

"Well, we can't have that." Nigel poured and handed her a cup. "My apologies about dropping the box," he said. "Cream? Sugar?"

"Pah!" she shot back. "I take it black. So, what am I doing here so dark and early?"

"This is Karen," I began. "She is a friend of Amanda's. Her seventeen-year-old son is a prisoner of some petty gangsters in a house on Baldwin. We are going to get him out this morning, and we need your help to create a diversion." I waited a few seconds for a reaction from her. Her only movement was to blink, so I continued. "We are going back to the house to put the squeeze on them. We've been in the house already and they treated us badly, twice."

"They beat the shit out of Michael," said Amanda from the laptop.

"Delicately put," said Nigel.

"And you're going back?" asked Tamara. "Why don't you call the police?"

"Not an option, at present," said Nigel calmly.

"Of course," replied Tamara mirroring the calm. "Okay, next."

"Once we are inside the house, we will demand they hand over the kid," I said. "We're quite hopeful they will comply, one way or another, but if they decline, we'll need a diversion to convince them we are not to be taken lightly. We thought if there were some bigger gangsters after us who, say, had followed us to the house on Baldwin, and perhaps we were subject to a drive-by shooting that might shake them up enough to forget the kid and run for it out the back door, while we make a getaway with Kyle in hand into the fake line of fire out the front door." I took a large pause. "We thought you might like to be that group of drive-by shooters." I stood looking at her, waiting for a reaction.

"This is good," she said without emotion. "The gunshots won't even be heard in the street because there is no gun out there." She had narrowed her eyes and was speaking quietly, almost to herself as if she were working out the logic. "The only pops will be inside the house from some wall-loaded squibs, and those will be enough to convince anyone in there that they're under fire." She paused and looked around at us all. Then she started nodding slowly and deeply. "I'm going to like working with you guys."

"He's made contact with the woman at the rave!" interrupted Amanda, reading the laptop screen.

"We're watching one of the gang guys via his Twitter feed," said Bid to Tamara. "We need to know where he is, so we can get the kid while the kingpin is away from the house. If he shows up at the house while we're there, we're done. We're watching his geotags."

Tamara gave her head a shake. "I have new respect for you guys. Are you sure you're actors?" she said. I looked over at Bid. It was the first time I had ever seen her laugh.

"So, let's get me embedded in this team," Tamara said as she opened one of the cases to reveal rows of multiple sealed compartments. "I'll need to know what kind of host these squibs are going into," she said to Bid.

"Right. Some will be body loads and some will go on the wall," Bid explained. "Michael, from what I can remember, the walls in the front foyer of the house were a mixture of materials. It looked like someone started to renovate at one time and then gave up. The wall that ran perpendicular to the door beside the palm tree was drywall. The wall on the other side was lath and plaster. Can you remember if the one facing the door was gypsum board or was it plaster?"

"I don't know," I said, trying to recall. "I was tied up on the floor in pain. I don't really remember."

"Were you facing that wall at any time?" asked Tamara, holding up a hand like a traffic cop. I nodded. "Were there any marks on the wall, like dents or chips out of it?"

"Yeah, there was a big chunk at the bottom of the door frame, and there were a few dents like a bowling ball hit it, and one hole right through, like an elbow had been rammed into it," I said. "It was chalky."

"Drywall," Bid and Tamara chorused. "That's good," continued Tamara, smiling. "Drywall is much easier to work with and easier to disguise than lath and plaster." She began to flip open some of the little compartments in the case.

"Colour of the wall?" asked Tamara.

"Whitish . . . like a dirty white," I said.

"Good," said Tamara.

"I can't say for sure though," I continued. "There wasn't much light in there."

"Even better," said Tamara as she held up one of the squibs. I had never seen one like it before. It was a very thin little cone with a tapered bottom that went to a silver point like a tack. It was about the same shape as a sharpened pencil end, only it was off-white. Out of the side of the flat top of the squib was a very long light-coloured wire, about as thin as fishing line.

"The silver pin at the bottom is what you jam into the wall," said Tamara. She walked over to my wall and stuck it in like a map pin. "Then use your thumb to press it as far in as it will go, like this." She demonstrated so that it was completely flush with the wall. It almost disappeared. "Don't worry if it doesn't go in all the way. They're pretty invisible, as you can see." She turned around and called me over. "Okay, your turn." I pushed one of the squibs into the wall beside the other. It made a slight crunch as it went in, but she was right. It was easy.

"It feels as if I were pushing in one of those yellow drywall plugs into a hole," I said looking at Nigel, "except, there's no need to drill a pilot hole. You try one." He did and nodded approvingly.

Tamara then pulled the three squibs out of my wall with a screwdriver and her fingernails, leaving three small, neat holes. I didn't even have time to complain about them. Bid was already at them with a yellow tube of wall plaster. She quickly filled the holes, licked her thumb, and smoothed them over. "We'll paint these in a few days when they are completely dry," she said to me as she dropped the tube back into her bag.

"Are you going to sneak into the house first to put in the squibs, or are you hoping they'll leave the room once you're in there?" Tamara asked.

"We don't know yet," said Nigel. "We're going to improvise."

"Improvise?" said Karen as if we'd said something bizarre. "You're guys are going to ad lib getting Kyle out?" She was getting ready to panic.

"Technically, ad-libbing and improvising are not the same thing," interrupted Nigel. I sensed he was going to begin a lecture on semantics, so I shot him a look to cut him short.

"What Nigel means is we are going to manage the situation," I said, trying to calm her down and help her understand. "We won't really know what the circumstances will be until we get there, but don't worry. Our lives are all about adapting to circumstances. Theatre people really think very well on their feet."

"And, remember, I have the cops on speed-dial," said Bid. Karen nodded. Bid turned back to Tamara. "So, what about the squibs?"

"When they're set off, they crack louder than you would expect, and there is a nice, good-size puff of cornstarch, which looks like smoke," answered Tamara. "In fact, the whole thing is made of cornstarch. They'll look great and they're environmentally friendly. Well, mostly."

"Are they numbered or labelled so we know in what order to place them?" asked Nigel.

"Don't worry about that, it won't matter. And from the sounds of it, you won't have time," said Tamara. "And once they start going off, your friends in there will be thinking about other things."

"The squibs will already be attached to the detonator pack when you go in," said Bid. "The detonator packs are radio controlled, both for your body and for the walls. The one for the wall is pretty small, but you'll still have to hide it somewhere. We'll make sure that the wires are long enough to allow you to hide it. Behind something on the floor is the best spot. I seem to remember there was a lot of junk lying around. Just put it by the baseboard, directly under where the squibs are set and kick something in front of it. The one on your body will be easy to hide under your clothes. Just make sure you leave the door open so we can see inside when we pull up in the van."

"Won't the wires be visible?" Nigel asked.

"Probably not. Here look at the wires." She held them against my wall." They're really fine and you guys said the lighting in that place is pretty dim. Your friends inside will be more concerned with you than their environment," said Bid. "There's so much clutter in that place that they won't notice some small difference, anyway. You will have to find an opportunity to get the squibs into the wall, though. That's up to you two." She indicated Nigel and me.

"Okay, get that shirt off," said Tamara. I must have hesitated. "Don't look at me like that."

"I'll give you a hand," said Nigel as he walked over to me. "Are you okay with the buttons?"

"Yeah, I seem to be feeling a bit better," I said, surprising even myself, while I flipped open the buttons.

"Did I miss something?" asked Tamara sarcastically while I let the shirt fall to the floor. "Has he become royalty in the last few hours? Nice tube-top she said, looking at the bandage around my midsection."

"I was quite tender before," I confessed. "But the Advil has helped." Nigel picked up my shirt.

"I want to have a look at your chest again and rewind that bandage," said Bid as she began to gently unwrap my torso. "It will be blue like this for a few days, maybe up to two weeks. How does it feel?"

"Chilly." Karen was looking like she would cry again so I said, "And with all of you staring at me I feel a bit objectified." I was taking shallow breaths to keep from moving my ribs. I didn't want to risk the sharp pains again.

"You're going to the doctor after this, right," Bid was not really asking. I nodded. She turned her attention the other way. "Tamara, do you want to have the squib guard over or under the bandage?"

"Over," she answered. "It's an all-in-one guard. You'll see when we get it on." Bid started to rewind the bandage on me while I held my arms up. Then Tamara said to me, "I'll put a guard on you so that when the squibs deploy, the back pressure doesn't bruise you, although," she looked at my blue chest, "who would know," she trailed off. "The guard looks a lot like this bandage, but it is lighter and wider and a little more rigid to disperse the pressure so that you won't be hurt."

Bid was making the bandage tighter this time to accommodate my walking around, and there was no knowing what other kind of activity I would be engaged in. She wanted to keep my chest as immobile as possible. Tamara gathered up Karen and Nigel, gave them each a pair of needle-nose pliers and showed them how to connect the squibs to the detonators by neatly splicing the tiny wires. They worked at that while Tamara went back to the tool boxes and flipped open a few other compartments. She held up a few small, peach-coloured domes that resembled small meringues or flattened nipple-less breasts. I knew they must be the body squibs because they had the telltale thin wires already attached.

Bid had finished with my bandage, so Tamara started to wind me up in the peach-coloured guard. The guard was like a bandage but wider and had a semi-rigid backing which sat against the skin. The front of it had many small slits that were actually little pockets. She started popping the little domes into these pockets, which stretched the slits open to leave the fronts of the squibs exposed. She was careful not to place them symmetrically. Then she moved around to my back and popped in a few there.

"How many are you putting on me?" I was a little worried. "Is this going to look like the toll booth scene in the *Godfather*?"

"We just need a few extras in case some don't go off," she said. "Sometimes we get misfires." Then she took my laundered shirt from the hanger and helped me put it on. She reached in and marked off a few places with pins that corresponded to the centre of the squibs. She collected a box that contained tiny triangular sequins from her tool box. She had a few different colours and matched one to the colour of my blue shirt. With thread the same colour as my shirt, she quickly sewed the blue sequins into the spots marked by pins on the inside of my shirt. With pins and other objects held in her mouth, she explained what she was doing.

"These are called shears," she said out of the side of her mouth while holding up a sequin. "The points are very sharp. I'll sew them into the shirt to keep them attached to the fabric so they'll hold on even after the squib is deployed. When the squib fires, the compressed air and stage blood are released very quickly and straight away from your body. It pushes the shear's point against the fabric, which creates a small rip allowing the air, cornstarch, and blood to escape. The air pressure rips it further. In the blink of an eye, the compressed air creates a bloody bullet hole from the inside. Clever, no?"

"Genius," I said sincerely. "Will I feel it?"

"You'll feel a quick pressure hit," she said while buttoning me up. "Well, you'll feel a few hits, but no pain. Okay, tuck it in. It works better if the fabric is nice and taut." She looked me over and then said, "This will be the last time you'll wear this shirt. Once these squibs detonate, your shirt will be toast. Now, I've put quite a few on you: some on your chest and some on your back. You won't have to worry about a thing from here on. Have you worn a squib before?"

"A few years ago," I said nervously. It wasn't a pleasant memory. "I had one on my thigh for a film. I got shot in the leg. It was a powder charge that sat over a steel plate and under a condom filled with blood."

"Whew!" she mocked. "That was back in the Stone Age. I don't use powder charges: too unstable. These are compressed air and the blood is built in. Okay," she continued, "so, you know then, that they'll take you by surprise, even if you think you're ready. This'll be a bit different than a single one on your leg, too. On your chest and back, these can be a bit frightening — er, I mean startling. We have no time for a rehearsal, so you won't know what it feels like until it happens, and you can't anticipate when they'll go, 'cause I'll be out of sight."

"That's probably better," I said, trying to make myself believe it. "My reaction will probably be more authentic that way."

135

"You can count on it," she said. "Now, I'll be watching. I'll be in the van outside the front door to keep it as safe as possible. I'll have my finger on the switch, but you'll have the final say."

Before I could even ask what she meant Bid went on, "One of you will have my Bluetooth headset in your pocket. We'll be listening over that, but the volume won't be great if it is sitting in your pocket. We might lose the connection for some reason. We'll need a hand signal as a backup." Then she said loudly so everyone could hear, "I need everyone to look in this direction. This is important."

Once she had everyone's attention she said, "Here are Michael's hand signals. It is important that everyone knows what they are, just in case. If you want to abort the gunshots, you'll put your hand behind you and open it flat." She demonstrated, turning so that everyone could see. "If you need the squibs to go earlier, make a fist behind your back. Very simple: open hand for stop and a fist if you want us to fire the shots immediately." She alternated a few times to make it clear.

"Let me see you do it," she said to me. We went through it a few times until she was satisfied I had it right.

Karen spoke up for the first time in a while. "What will keep the gang from seeing us if we can see them through the front door when we drive up?"

"What do you mean 'we'?" asked Amanda. "You're not going to be there."

"To hell with that," said Karen pointing at Amanda with her pliers. "This is my son! I'm going to be there. What if they see us?" she said again firmly.

"OK, you're right. Of course you should be there. They won't see us because as soon as we drive up, we will be shining a very bright spotlight into the front door," said Amanda. "It won't blind them, but they won't be able to see anything outside the door. We'll only drive up and shine the light when we are about to start the gunfire, right Bid?"

"Right. Amanda will be on the wheel. Karen, since you're coming, you'll be on the light, and Tamara, of course, will be on the detonators," said Bid. "I am stage management; I will call the show." No one argued because it was only natural.

"Oh, and don't forget to make sure that the door is open so we can see those signals," said Tamara.

"How's our boy Sal?" asked Nigel looking up from the table, pliers in hand.

"I think he's going to win that dare," said Amanda. "God, she must be stupid," meaning the girl Sal had hooked up with.

A door slammed in the hallway. My heart leapt up into my mouth. I looked over at my front door and saw that we had forgotten to close it when Tamara came in. My next door neighbour Dennis was on his way outside for his early morning walk with his two white teacup poodles, Casey and Finnegan. He was surprised to see me with an apartment full of guests, and paused to say hello.

"Good morning," he said looking impressed. "You're up early . . . or late. I thought you actors never got up early."

"Late," I said looking apologetic. "We're rehearsing something new and we were working on a scene. I guess the time just got away from us."

Dennis was a bus driver for the Transit Commission. His shift started at six every morning, so he was up early enough to take "the boys," as he called them, out for their morning stroll at around three-thirty. The walk usually didn't last long. More often than not, he ended up carrying the tiny dogs back, one nestled in the crook of each arm. He had about an hour's commute to start his bus route, so he left at about four-thirty. I rarely saw him at the beginning of his day. Most often, I would see him as I left for work at the theatre, when he was coming back from his shift at four in the afternoon.

"When does this show open?" he asked shifting his gaze to Nigel.

"Me?" Nigel was startled. "Oh . . . er, another two weeks."

Dennis looked back at me. "If you have any tickets without a good home, remember your neighbour." He took a long uncomfortable look at me with a critical eye. "Are you putting on weight for this role?" He said as he playfully poked me in the belly with an index finger. "What's this?" He bounced his finger on my padded stomach a few times.

"I'm experimenting with a little something extra around the middle for the role I'm working on right now." I was trying not to lie.

"Hmm," he mused, making a disapproving face. "I'll have to wait to see if it is effective in the show. That is, if you come through with a ticket for me. If not, I may come looking for you," he said with a large toothy smile to Nigel, while throwing a hand out in greeting. "We haven't been introduced. I'm Dennis."

"Er . . . Nigel," said Nigel sheepishly. "A pleasure. A ticket? Yes, by all means, just let me know."

Dennis was enjoying himself. Then he must have noticed the scar on Nigel's neck, and caught himself staring, because he quickly turned his attention to the dogs who were prone like miniature polar bear rugs, as only poodles can. "Come on boys, let's go out and squeeze a kidney." The two dogs leapt up and danced along the hall and down the stairs after him.

I closed the door and turned around. Nigel stood behind me looking embarrassed, shaking his head and rolling his eyes. Amanda smirked at him. Tamara, oblivious, carefully wound up the squibs for transport.

138

"Thirty minutes, please," said Bid. "This is your half-hour call."

There was a sizzling sound and the glorious smell of hot butter coming from the kitchen. Karen had set out plates and cutlery and was frying something.

"I'm cooking omelettes," she said. "No one here has eaten anything since yesterday except coffee and Scotch. You cannot go out there this morning without eating. Michael, you had all the right ingredients for omelettes . . . but nothing else."

For the next twenty minutes or so, we ate in relative silence while we each pondered the roles we would play. The dishes were done and stacked away and Bid announced, "Okay, let's go."

"He's on the move!" chirped Amanda, her eyes glued to the laptop.

"Where?" asked Nigel.

"A Tim's on the Danforth," said Amanda.

"How far east?"

"I'll look it up in Maps," she said. After a few seconds she said, "Victoria Park."

"That's good and far," said Nigel. "Keep an eye on him. Bring the laptop and let's go."

"Whoa!" I said realizing that we'd hit a snag. "The laptop won't work in the van."

"Crappy battery?" asked Nigel.

"No — no network connection," I said. "We can't access the Web and his Twitter account without the Web."

"I can apply to his Twitter account to follow him from my phone," said Karen. "That would work."

"No good," Bid said, throwing a monkey wrench in. "If he is smart, he will have set his settings to approve any follows. Then he would be able to track you and find out who you were. He is vain enough to have set it to be notified when he is being followed. That

139

means he could identify you using your account. Sorry, no go. The only way to do it anonymously is using a computer on the Web."

"We could try to access a free wireless connection on Baldwin," said Nigel. "It's a pretty high-density area. Surely, someone must be running an unprotected wireless hub there, somewhere."

"Do you want to take a chance on it?" said Bid.

"Doesn't anyone here have one of those wireless sticks that the phone companies sell?" asked Tamara.

"Dennis does!" I realized. "I saw him use it on his laptop this summer outside on the front stoop. He said he felt like a Beach Boy surfing in the sun." I hurried next door and knocked. There was no answer. He was still out with the boys, so I left my door open and we waited to catch him on the way back in.

The cat must have let her curiosity get the better of her. She crawled out from under the couch and looked at all of us suspiciously before creeping, with her belly almost on the floor, toward the front door. She sat looking at the empty space in the hallway for a few seconds, and closed her eyes while flattening her ears sideways.

"Aren't you afraid the cat'll take off?" asked Tamara.

"I'm not that lucky," I said. The cat lay down in front of the door facing out, while we all waited quietly. Suddenly she shot straight back and flew under the couch again.

"Dennis is back," I said.

"I don't hear anything," said Amanda.

"Me either," said Bid.

"You will. The cat has radar," I said, "and she hates those dogs. It'll be Dennis, you'll see."

Sure enough, we heard the door creak open downstairs followed by his slow footsteps on the staircase. As he rounded the corner he must have wondered why we were all in the doorway staring at him as he stood there startled, his arms full of dogs. "They get tired," he said smiling, trying to explain. "Short legs."

"Dennis, I need your help." We must have all looked desperate, because he responded with an equally urgent look on his face.

"Sure, what do you need?"

"Your Internet — USB stick — thing," I said not knowing what to call it.

"Yeah, sure," he said suspiciously. "Is your Internet not working? I can help you out with that when I get home from work this afternoon."

"No, my network is fine," I said. "I just need to be mobile for a few hours and I need Web access while I'm out. I'll pay for any access fees and I promise not to stick you with a big bill . . . and I'll get it back to you as soon as you come home this afternoon."

"Yeah, sure," he said again slowly, looking at us first tentatively, then guardedly, clearly wondering what we were up to. No one else had said a thing, but they were all staring at him with pleading eyes.

"You know, you're going to love this new show," Nigel piped up to break the tension. "Forget about Michael's ticket. My tickets are better. You'll be my guest."

Dennis was already reaching into his pocket and pulled out the USB stick. "I always carry it with me," he said. He almost sounded embarrassed. "You just plug it into your USB port and follow the prompts." I could see that he had a few questions forming.

Bid had already reached between us, taken it out of his hand, and disappeared behind us again into my apartment, before he had quite finished.

"Dennis, thanks," said Karen genuinely, taking his hands in hers. "This is very important to us. I am very grateful." I am sure he was wondering who the hell she was, but he had no chance to ask.

"Okay! We're in!" snapped Bid from across my living room. She had successfully installed the stick and accessed the Web. "Let's saddle up!"

Amanda was the first out, squeezing between us and walking with the laptop held in front of her at eye level, the power cord swagged around her neck and the USB stick poking out the back like a divining rod pointing the way. As she scooted through the door, and right by Dennis, she announced, "He's on the move again — Vic Park and Eglinton — another donut shop." Dennis visibly straightened.

"He must have it set to check in automatically," said Tamara as she followed Amanda past Dennis and through the door.

"Were you not here when we already talked about that?" asked Nigel right behind her.

"I'm confirming it, smart ass," she said, lugging the tool boxes and the trolley behind her. "Grab the bottom end when we reach the stairs."

"With pleasure," said Nigel with a wink to me.

"Don't make me hurt you," Tamara threatened without missing a beat.

Bid said, "Karen, you'll have to hold on to these till we get downstairs." She was holding up the squibs and detonators. "Don't fold them or wind them up, and try not to bang them around. I'll take them from you when we get to the van." Karen took them and walked toward the stairs as if they were made of nitroglycerin, holding them high so the ends wouldn't touch the ground. Bid followed, laden with a number of heavy bags. I locked my apartment door and spun around to see Dennis still there staring wide-eyed at me.

"I can't wait to hear about this later," he said calmly with his eyebrows raised. "My first impulse is to try to wrench it out of you now, but I've got a feeling this is a long story and I've got to get to work." He exhaled loudly as he opened his door to deposit the boys back inside his apartment. "This is going to eat at me all day, you know."

Chapter 17

To say the van was a bit crowded would be a gross understatement. We were packed in like a clown car. There were originally seven seats in the van and only six of us, but we had far more equipment and gear than anticipated. The trunk area was mostly taken up with a large cardboard box that held the fake pills. We had to remove one of the seats in the middle section by the sliding door, and Nigel ran that back upstairs to my apartment. The space left behind would accommodate the two who would operate from the van: Karen with the light and Tamara with the wireless detonator switches. Our equipment had to be ready to use and close at hand in case we needed it. To avoid tangling, the squibs were hung from the grab handles where the explosive ends sat draped carefully by Tamara's seat. Amanda drove, and Bid rode shotgun, frequently checking the open laptop on her knees. Bid had plugged in a device that converted the DC power from the cigarette lighter in the van to AC power for the laptop, because I did, apparently, have a crappy battery. It was dangerously low just from the walk downstairs to the van.

"Start the van," said Bid. "This laptop's power is going south in a hurry. We need the engine running to keep it charged." There were two outlets in the power supply. She plugged the hand-held spotlight into the other one.

I was hunched over and making my way to the far back seat where Nigel was already sitting at the left. I sat on the right and forward a bit so as not to disturb the body packs just under my shirt. I also didn't want to crush the detonator hidden just behind my belt, where Tamara wanted it positioned so she could be sure of a clear signal when she pulled the trigger, so to speak. She figured my back would be towards her at the critical moment. The spotlight rested lens down on the floor by the sliding door. Karen squeezed in between Nigel and me. She was insisting on doing up her seatbelt, but because her spot was in the middle, she was having a hard time finding the belt. When she couldn't find it with probing fingers next to Nigel, she got impatient and hurriedly swung around to look for it next to me. That's when her elbow connected at full speed with my side.

Up to that point I had thought my ribs were feeling better. It might have been the Advil or because I had begun to favour my ribs by walking a little stooped, neglecting to move my neck and head in an attempt to minimize my movement as well, so the pain had subsided to a dull throb — just tender enough to remind me to treat my ribs with care and to move gently. Karen wasn't receiving the same message though, and as her elbow caught me square in the middle, renewed pain shot through me, and I thought I would throw up. I instinctively pulled my arms in to guard against a replay and I stopped breathing, hoping that even less movement might mean less pain. I was wrong. I felt like I was being knifed. As Karen straightened, she jostled me again, throwing me deeper into agony.

Karen looked like she was witnessing a murder. Her eyes and mouth opened wide and she shot out the tips of her fingers in my direction, as though that might be a soothing gesture. I took it to mean she was going to touch me again and recoiled, only to be stopped dead by the van's side window behind me. A shriek of pain ran through my entire body when I pulled away from her, accompanied by a sharp popping feeling. I must have let out a scream commensurate with the pain, though I don't recall it, because everyone in the van turned in terror to look at me. The only sounds for a few seconds were Karen gasping, and somewhere down the block, a dog barking. Everyone else had stopped breathing.

I can't explain what happened with any real authority. I only know that as of that moment, after the pop, the sharp pain in my side stopped. The bruised feeling was there, but that was nothing compared to what I had been suffering. I could only speculate the kicking I had taken earlier must have dislocated a rib, not broken it, and the jostling in the back seat of the van had popped it back into place.

"I'm okay," I said to Karen, probably a bit too urgently. She refused to move, her fingers still stretched toward me like she was a witch stopped in mid-spell. There was nowhere to go anyway in the confines of the back seat. Nigel slowly leaned forward to look around Karen's behind to see me.

"Oh — my — God!" started Karen.

"No really, I'm better. There's no pain at all. You must have popped it back into place," I said, while slowly sinking back down into the seat. "I think you did me a favour, actually." I was afraid the pain was only hiding, though, and would rear its ugly head. I carefully tested my ribs by turning gingerly from side to side and poking myself with my fingers. I was tender, but I was much better.

"All right. If you three stooges are quite finished, we'll be off," said Bid over her shoulder. Then she said to Amanda, "Hit it," and we pulled away from the curb.

146

That was as far as the concrete portion of our plan had taken us: to the van. It was still dark out, but the sun would soon rise I thought; although, I was no expert on anything to do with early mornings. We knew where we were going and we had a sketch of a plan, but really, from here on in, we were flying by the seat of our pants.

It wasn't a long drive over to Baldwin, so there was a flurry of chatter on the way there to try and flesh out a strategy. The upshot was Nigel and I would go in, place the squibs, and talk to the gang. We would demand Kyle and get him downstairs. If they didn't release him to us, the shooting would start, and when the Pack Boys ran for cover we would head into the bogus line of fire, taking Kyle with us. At the same time, Bid and Karen would spread the counterfeit dope onto the lawn, stairs, and through the doors to give the police something to go into the house for. The last thing we would do is grab the spent squibs from the wall, after running into the bogus crossfire with Kyle, run to the van, and take off while Bid called the police.

It was 4:20 a.m. when we made our first pass in front of the house on Baldwin. We took it slowly, but not suspiciously so. Bid wanted to assess what we were up against. She called it a *recky*. Only Nigel was brave enough to ask her what she was talking about.

"Reconnoitre," she said. Even though she was in the front seat, and I could only see the back of her head, I could tell she was rolling her eyes.

Most of the lights were on in the house, but there was no movement to be seen from the outside. The blue Honda was there on the parking pad and the street was empty of people, but cars were parked all the way up the street on both sides. Amanda drove us right by the house and we turned the corner to go around the block. On the way up the street I scanned the parked cars. There was no sign of Sal's BMW. When we'd reached the corner of Baldwin again, Bid said in a lowered voice, "Let's park here and get ourselves ready to go. Roll down all the windows," she added.

We had to park right at the corner and switch off the van so the running lights wouldn't attract attention. For a few minutes, we listened to the crackling sound of the cooling engine tinkling like a wind chime.

"This isn't going to get any easier, if we just sit and wait," Amanda said quietly. "Let's decide on the action."

"Nigel will carry the squibs under his long coat until we get inside," I said. "Then, he'll get the coat off at the first chance he has, and we'll lodge them into the wall." Nigel nodded.

I started to move forward out of my seat to climb out of the van when Amanda hissed, "Freeze!" Every actor knows this command. It doesn't mean just stop; it literally means freeze the action exactly where it is. I was looking forward through the front windshield with my back bent, and I could see someone had exited through the front door of the house. He stood on the porch for a second or two and stretched, raising his arms high above his head. He was carrying something small, about the size of a shoebox. He pointed a fist at the Honda and chirped the alarm before heading down the steps and getting in. It looked like it might have been Skinny, but it was too dark and we were too far up the block to tell for sure.

Bid was slowly folding the laptop screen down so that our faces wouldn't be illuminated in the dark. Even though we were almost a block away, she didn't want to take any chances. I saw the tail light of the Honda blink on and heard the engine whine to life. It bumped off the parking pad, onto the street, and purred away for a few metres before we heard the muffled thumping of the music start, and then fade away as the tail lights got smaller and turned the corner. He drove like he wasn't in a rush.

Bid flipped open the laptop again and lowered the brightness settings to slightly mute the light from the screen. "He's moving again," she whispered. "A pharmacy on Danforth, near Victoria Park. I hope he's being responsible. No . . . Looks like he's dropped that girl off, too. He is tweeting 'Jackpot, looks even better naked. I'm done and gone and hungry. You owe me!' Ugh, he's a pig," she groaned.

"We've got to move now," I said. "He may start to head over here."

With the squibs draped around his neck, Nigel hid the wires inside his long coat. He also had Bid's Bluetooth headset in his ear to stay in contact until we reached the house, when he was to slip it into his pocket.

As I stepped out of the van, I saw Tamara take out a small box that looked like a video game controller. "Wait," she said. "Let me turn on the controller before you go." The tiny light blinked red a few times and then went to a solid green. "It's made a wireless connection with the detonator. It's armed. Don't worry, the safety is on."

We briskly, and almost, silently walked up the street. Nigel muttered, "Merde."

"Break a leg," is what I answered.

I could not believe I was going to be back in that house for the third time in twenty-four hours. The last two times I had been taken by surprise, thumped on the head, and either thrown out back like hazardous waste, or tied up like a rolled brisket and then tenderized. I wasn't going in blind this time. There were windows on the ground floor and I was going to make use of them to see if anyone was lounging in the foyer with a baseball bat in their hands, or worse. I asked Nigel to wait at the walkway to the next house while I had a closer look.

Although light escaped from inside through the opaque curtains covering the window to the right of porch, I could see nothing. The window on other side of the porch offered a small enough gap between the curtains to see that the foyer was empty. The small baseball bat still stood in the coat rack.

"It's all quiet in there," I whispered to Nigel when I reached him. "I have an idea."

"Wait," he said looking down and his head cocked slightly left. He was listening to Bid through her Bluetooth earpiece. "Bid wants to know what's going on. Stand closer to me and talk into the mic so she can hear too."

"There's no one in the front hall," I whispered into the mic. "You stay here until I get back. I'll sneak in, set the squibs, and come back here. Then we'll bang on the door together."

"Bid says, what if it's locked?" Nigel translated.

"Then we just go and bang on the door," I said. "But I didn't see them lock the door before when I was in there, and when that guy drove away just a few minutes ago, he didn't lock the door, either."

"Amanda says forget it, just follow the plan," Nigel said flatly.

"Amanda has given me bad advice twice before," I said, trying to make light of it and speaking very close to the mic. "I like it this way. Give me the squibs."

Nigel began transferring the squibs over his head and onto my shoulders as if he was passing on an award when he said, "You've created a lot of controversy on the other end of this thing." He pointed at the earpiece. "They're debating your sanity."

"They wouldn't be the first," I said. "Wait here. This shouldn't take long." At that moment a car came down the street. Nigel quickly grabbed me in his arms and bear-hugged me, burying his head in my neck. The car passed without stopping or slowing down.

"What?" He said into the microphone as he released me. "No, I just gave Michael a good luck kiss." Then he said to me, "Sorry to be so forward. Two guys loitering on the street at four thirty may look suspicious, but two people kissing is no cause for suspicion. Now, go!" he mouthed.

"You owe me for that," I said.

"How about dinner?" he suggested as I slunk toward the front door, waving him off over my shoulder.

I climbed up the porch steps as quietly as possible. A small creak was enough to set off my butterflies but hopefully not alarm anyone inside. I walked crouched over to keep from casting a silhouette on the door's frosted window. The door was unlocked, as expected, and as I carefully turned the handle to open the door, I took a look back at Nigel, who was slipping behind a large tree by the street. I was inside in a flash, listening for any sound that would present a threat. All was quiet, except for the pounding of my heart.

I walked around the perimeter of the room, close to the walls to avoid any squeaking floorboards, and I grabbed the baseball bat on my way by the coat rack. I had no plans for it, but I didn't want it to find its way into anyone else's hands, either. I carefully opened the door to the room where I had been kept prisoner earlier and silently lay the bat on the floor to keep it out of sight. The small room looked different from this angle. I could see the underside of the stairs above and judging by some old plumbing that had been roughly cut off, this had undoubtedly been a powder room at one time. I pulled the door not quite closed so there would be no noise of the latch clicking home. One by one I unwound the squibs from my neck and pressed them into the wall in a pattern that I hoped would appear random, was not too linear and not too close together. The squibs made a bigger crunching sound as they went into the wall than I had anticipated, so I tried to push them in slowly to keep the noise down. Tamara was right about the wires. In this light and even at this close distance, they were almost invisible. But the detonator, which was the size of a matchbox, would be sorely out of place if left to just sit on the floor. I looked around the littered hallway for something to conceal the detonator. A small empty tissue box further down the hallway by the wall was perfect. As I went to retrieve it I stepped on a floorboard that didn't creak as much as it trumpeted a fanfare. My heart jumped into my mouth and I froze, but there was no answering noise from upstairs. I reached for the box to quickly cover the detonator and saw the rag that had been stuffed into my mouth earlier. I threw that over the top of the detonator, too.

Everything I did now seemed to sound louder than it should. My heart was racing and my adrenaline was flowing like Niagara. I knew I needed to get out right away, and as I took the first step toward the front door, I heard a sound that made me want to break into a run: a door slammed upstairs. The footsteps already thumping down the stairs were quick and heavy. The stairs commanded a good view of the front door. If I were to run for the front door, I'd be caught for sure and our entire plan would be ruined. So, without much thought, I ducked into the old powder room, my former prison, and as I caught the rhythm of the footsteps, I clicked the door closed on one of the footfalls. I lowered myself in the dark to my old position of lying on the floor so I could see through the door's low woven panel.

I recognized Burly's fat ankles as he made his way to the centre of the foyer, facing away from me and toward the front door. As he walked to the centre of the hall, I could see him check the room. He paused there for a few seconds, yawned, and then took a few steps toward the front door. He must have been asleep and my banging about woke him. He paused with his hand on the front doorknob for a moment and then pulled it open. I could feel the cool night air through the scrim and watched him stand in the archway and stretch.

152

He reached high as he stretched. His T-shirt rode up on his midsection, exposing a roll of blubber on his back that folded over the sides of his worn, white cotton underpants, hiding parts of the elastic waist band. His beltless jeans rode low on his hips, exposing his pale buttocks through almost diaphanous underwear. He reached a pinnacle of disgusting when he broke wind in mid-stretch.

There I was, trapped and lying on the floor, with him between me and safety. I was willing him to go back upstairs, when I saw him glance at the coat rack. He looked in the other direction too, at the potted palm, and then back at the coat rack a little more urgently. He was looking for something. The bat! I moved my right hand and felt the baseball bat I had laid there. I started to fear this wasn't going to go the way we intended. I felt my hand curl around the bat, ready to do whatever was necessary to get out and get the kid upstairs to safety. Burly turned and tentatively headed for my hideout. My adrenaline surged and my grip tightened on the bat as I rose to my knees, about to stand before he would open the door. I was prepared to deliver the surprise of his life. But he stopped suddenly and swung back toward the front door, where Nigel stood on the threshold, smiling.

"Having a late night . . . or an early morning?" Nigel asked cheerily.

"Wha?" Burly was clearly not a morning person. I was back down on my belly watching the scene play out in the hall.

"I'm here to pick him up," said Nigel quickly and confidently. "Is he ready to go?"

"What?" Burly actually shook his head a few times as if to reboot his brain like an Etch A Sketch. "Go where? And who, the fuck, are you talking about?"

Nigel was obviously talking about Kyle, but I didn't like the sound of this. What if they had already moved him? Or what if he hadn't been there at all?

"The kid, upstairs," said Nigel. "I'm supposed to pick him up. Why don't you check to see if he's ready? Sal said he'd be ready by now." Nigel looked at his watch as if to confirm this was indeed the agreed upon time, and then he shrugged and nodded.

Burly was priceless. His neck actually straightened as if a thought had finally entered his head.

"All right I'll look, but . . ." he trailed off and then headed upstairs again with much more laboured steps than he took on the way down. When I heard a door close upstairs, I opened the powder room door and faced Nigel.

"Get out," he mouthed at me while violently waving his hand toward the door. As I passed him he whispered, "Wait a few minutes and then come back in."

I ran outside and hid behind the tree he had used for cover a few minutes before. I stood there trying to catch my breath, and wondering how long I should wait, when a tap on my shoulder made me jump. I sprung around prepared to face an assailant. I was holding the bat up high, ready to knock one out of the park, and looking straight into Bid's eyes while she held a cellphone up to her ear.

"What the hell is going on?" she yelled in a whisper. "And what are you doing with that bat?"

"I got trapped in a room hiding from one of them. He woke up and came down to see what was going on. He didn't see me though," I said proudly.

"And the bat?"

"The bat? . . . Shit . . . I don't know." I was as shocked as she was about the bat. I was still holding it ready to strike, so I lowered it. "I have to get back in there."

"Not yet," she said, grabbing hold of my sleeve and pulling back while still holding the phone up to her ear with the other hand. She was listening to the Bluetooth headset over her phone. "Nigel is still okay. That guy hasn't come back down yet. Now, settle down. It's important for you to know that we don't have much time. Sal's on the move again, and he is heading closer to us. I don't know if he is coming here or going home, wherever that is. He's made a stop on Cherry Street near the lake, but each stop he has made is bringing him closer to us. Worst case scenario is he'll be here in fifteen minutes."

"He must have stopped at the storage place," I said to her. "He won't be there long: a few minutes at the most."

"Wait," she said as her eyes flicked to the right where she held the cellphone up to her ear. "Nigel has just tapped the headset in his pocket in a shave-and-a-haircut rhythm. You had better go. . . . Be careful." She put her hand on my arm and squeezed. Then she turned and silently ran back to the parked van.

I thumped up the steps noisily, looking at Nigel's back through the open door. I wanted to make sure Nigel heard me coming. He looked around to see me. Burly reached the bottom step inside the house and started walking toward Nigel as I came over the threshold. He saw me walk in and said, "Where'd you come from?"

"Parking the car," I lied hoping he couldn't read the lie in my face. "So, are we going? Where's the kid?"

"Just what I'm trying to find out from our friend here," said Nigel to me. Then he turned his attention to Burly. "So, where is he?"

Burly took a look at my hand and was alarmed to see the baseball bat. His expression suggested he was trying to figure out how I could have just walked in and be holding the bat in my hand. He looked back at Nigel.

"Where is he?" Nigel asked again, this time aggressively.

"The kid's upstairs, but Sal didn't say nothin' about givin' him to you two." He must have been alone in the house, except for Kyle, of course.

"It's part of our arrangement," said Nigel. "Be a good lad and fetch him down."

I imagine that in addition to Nigel's tone and there being two of us, the fact that I had a baseball bat in my hand almost had him convinced. I think I saw a flicker of acceptance in his otherwise vacant expression, but then, as always happens with the best laid plans, it all started to go sideways.

Chapter 18

I thought I had heard it soon after I crossed the threshold, but of course, as with other ambient city sounds, I chose to block it out. A whining hum began in the distance: that distinctive sound of a low-slung, tricked-out economy car with headers, shifting gears. As it got grew closer I heard the thumping of the car stereo, too. I didn't become alarmed until I heard the blue Honda pull up on the parking pad behind us and the stereo and the motor go silent. All we were momentarily left with was that crackling sound of the engine cooling, until the car door opened and slammed. I wasn't going to be taken by surprise again, so I turned around just enough to see Skinny walking toward the house.

I tried to take the situation in hand by being pre-emptive with Burly, "Get him," I said, pointing at the stairs, meaning Kyle.

"Who?" answered Burly.

"The kid," I said, taking a step forward. "Get him now!"

Burly lumbered up the inside stairs again, and disappeared just as Skinny started up the outside stairs to the front door. At any other time, I would have described Skinny's expression as comical: his eyes were uncharacteristically wide in surprise, but his sphincter-like mouth was still clamped shut. He stomped up the stairs, his arms held out from his hips, almost like a gunfighter, to try to appear larger. The effect was only absurd. I leaned on the bat and stuck a hand in my pocket to make myself look less threatening. I could feel the receipts and the Tic Tacs from Friday's rehearsal — Friday seemed like a lifetime ago. Karen must have put them back where she had found them when she had my clothes cleaned.

"Hey!" squeaked Skinny when he walked in. "W'da' fuck's goin' on?"

Nigel took a breath to start to say something, but I cut him off with, "I need some water."

"What?" asked Skinny. Nigel's face posed the same question.

"I need some water to take my medication." I was holding up two Tic Tacs from my pocket.

Without missing a beat, Skinny headed to the other room. It was almost too easy. A car horn tooted lightly from down the block. Nigel looked at me.

"Is that horn for us?" Nigel whispered to me. *Toot-toot*, came the reply. He tapped his pocket quickly three times where the Bluetooth headset was. The result was three tiny toots from down the block. He fumbled for the headset in his pocket and jammed it to his ear. "What?" he said in a jagged whisper.

"Okay, okay!" he growled quietly and then stuffed the headset back into his pocket. "Shit!" he hissed at me. "We have less than five minutes; Sal is passing the Eaton Centre." I felt my heart sink into my bowels.

In fact, it wasn't five minutes; it was more like twenty seconds. There must have been a delay between the time the geotagging program checked in his location, and the time it appeared on the Web. That would be useful information in the future, but right now it was no use. Sal pulled up to the curb in his black car, and then gently bumped up and on to the parking pad while we stood watching just inside the open doorway. Burly must have heard both the Honda pull up and Sal's car arrive because he came back down empty-handed just as Sal walked through the doorway wearing an unuttered question on his face.

"Sorry Sal," apologized Burly. "I was doin' it, but then I heard your car, so . . ."

"Doing what?" then Sal turned to Nigel. "Robert, what're you doing here at this time of night?"

"Morning," I said correcting him. He looked back at me a little shocked that I had spoken out of turn. "Despite the fact that you have been out all night and lost track of time when you took that floozy home for a bit of horizontal tango, it's now morning. Don't bother asking again what we're doing here," I said putting up a hand to stop what looked like another question. "We want that kid, and we want him now." I figured that a full frontal attack would put them off balance and they might cave in, but Sal was tougher than that.

"No chance," he said. "He's mine and I have a score to settle with him. I want to find out who supplies him and then I want him out of my way. Punks like him don't understand polite talk. I didn't have the time to deal with him properly before, but now that he's been here for a while, he'll be softened up a bit and I've got more time to play. He'll tell me what I need to know." Then he twigged. "How'd you know about that girl?"

"I think you underestimate the length of my reach and the size of my organization," said Nigel. "There's not much about your actions tonight that we don't know. I know what time you left the bar and what time you stopped at Vic Park and Danforth. I know the route you took to the storage unit on Cherry Street and that you passed the Eaton Centre on the way here."

"Were you following me?" He didn't wait for an answer. He turned and blasted at Burly. "When did they get here?"

"About twenty minutes ago, Sal," said Burly. "He never left neither."

"Then how could he know all that stuff?" Sal was clearly shaken.

Skinny walked in with a bottle of water and handed it to me. He looked at Sal with a puzzled expression.

"Just get the kid," I said as evenly and threateningly as I could muster, "or we'll shut you down."

"Fuck you!" said Sal a little too loudly. He was starting to panic. Burly took this as his cue to rush me, but I'd had my eye on him and I was ready. A play I had done a few years before gave me what I needed to fend him off.

I had done extensive training in stage fighting: lots of sword work, rapier and dagger, some broadsword, and loads of hand-to-hand combat. I had been lucky enough to have worked with the country's premier stage combat instructor, Clay Border. When I had done Shakespeare's *Henry V*, Border trained me in quarterstaff fighting.

It all came back to me in an instant, so when Burly charged me, I merely had to raise the bat horizontally across my body and thrust it right, plunging the bat's end into his midsection. Despite the rather large cushion of his gut, it winded him and Burly went down like a bag of rice, rolling on the floor and gasping for air. I knew he would recover quickly, though, so we had to move fast. Skinny just threw up his hands in surrender and stepped back.

While I was watching Skinny, Sal made a grab for the bat. I was so pleased with having decked Burly that I was surprised by Sal, who wrenched the bat out of my hands. He took a step backward to keep me at bay and started to wind up for a swipe. As the bat made a horizontal arc, I leaned back. I felt the swish of air as it swung close by my face. He had taken such a large swing, though, that his follow-through took him right around landed him facing the other way. Burly, still winded but now livid, was starting to get up. Sal started to wind up again, doing what we in the stage fighting business call telegraphing: letting your fighting partner know where the next blow is coming. He hadn't even reached the apex of his swing when I let the plastic water bottle fly at him with all my might, hitting him square in the face. He went down on his back, dropping the bat, but was quickly on his feet again, looking for it. He didn't have a chance at the bat, though. Burly and Skinny were on the floor wrestling over it. Burly won through brute strength and used it to help him stand. Sal grabbed the coat rack, picking it up and trying to wield it as a weapon, but it was too large and he ended up gouging a wall with its base as he tried to swing at Nigel.

The water bottle on the floor had rolled back to lay by my feet, so I scooped it up. I was going to throw it at Skinny, who was starting to look braver, when I noticed my shadow on the back wall. Skinny narrowed his eyes, as did Sal, who dropped the coat rack and threw up his hands to shade his eyes from a bright light which came from behind me. There were a few loud bangs and pieces of plaster flew out of the back wall. Sal and his boys froze, bug-eyed.

Then I felt a stinging thump in my back as I involuntarily lurched around one hundred and eighty degrees to face the door. I was blinded by the white light coming from outside. I heard two more bangs and then some more plaster hit the floor.

"Shit!" Sal said. "He's been hit!" He must have been looking at my back.

That would probably have been enough, but Tamara was thorough in her work. My chest exploded twice. I saw the pop of the cornstarch rocket out from my chest, and my shirt tore perfectly with the fake

161

blood spraying straight out and onto the wall for the whole gang to see. I wasn't entirely sure that I hadn't really been shot. What made the whole thing perfect, though, was that because I was not expecting the second shot, as a reflex I shot out my arms. In doing so, I threw the water bottle aside and dislocated my rib again, sending me into fresh agony. I went down, crashing over the coat rack that lay on the ground, which added to the staged drama and to even more genuine pain in my midsection.

I must have screamed very persuasively, because Sal yelled, "It's the bikers, they've found us." They were convinced. The three of them flew out of the room, presumably toward the back door. A crashing sound in the other room confirmed it for me, but Nigel followed to sneak a look.

"They're gone. Nice job," said Nigel on his way back into the foyer. "You were a bit coarse, though evidently, convincing."

I started to try to get to my feet, but it was heavy going. I had to untangle myself from the coat rack with only one hand, while bracing my rib with the other. The pain in my chest felt like torture. Nigel reached down to give me a hand up and when he pulled, my rib shrieked back into place once more.

"They may come back soon; let's get Kyle," I gasped. "I don't want to have to come back here." Nigel and I leapt up the stairs to find three rooms with closed doors. The first door was locked, so I whacked out one of the wooden panels on the door with the bat. I reached in and unlocked the door from the inside. The room was floor to ceiling with white cardboard boxes labelled RunPharma. There was nothing else there so we left it. The next room had a few cots, some empty pizza boxes and beer cans, but nothing else. The last room was completely empty, too; no Kyle.

There was a noise downstairs and then I heard Bid yell, "Are you all right?"

"We're fine!" answered Nigel. "I'll go down," he said to me. "Keep looking!" and he sped off.

This was too much. After all that had happened, Kyle wasn't here. How could we have gotten it wrong? But it struck me: they had definitely acknowledged he was here; Burly had come up to fetch him down before Sal had showed up. He must be here somewhere. The only other place to look was the bathroom. He wasn't in there either. The place was filthy and had a stack of pizza delivery paper napkins jammed in where the toilet paper should have been. There were cigarette butts and burn stains in the sink and the toilet would be enough to make a housefly gag. On my way out, I noticed a rope by the latch side of the doorframe was tied off on a cleat in the wall and went straight up through a small hole in the ceiling. Curious, I untied it, and as it came loose, it offered resistance, so I let it out slowly and down came a small stairway in the hall. It rested over the other stairs and in the opposite direction. This new stairway came down in such a way that I couldn't go downstairs to the bottom floor and no one could come up, although I could see between them and saw Nigel appear at the foot of the other stairs below.

"What's up?" he asked urgently.

"The attic I think," I said. "I'll find out."

"You had better hurry," said Nigel. "They'll most likely be back soon. Bid and Tamara are gathering the spent wall squibs."

It was almost pitch dark in the attic. The only light filtered in from the hole where the small staircase opened up the floor. The space smelled of dust and mould.

"Kyle?" I tried. No answer. I felt around in the centre with my feet, but found nothing. As I carefully made my way to the far end with my hands out to keep me from bumping into anything, the old dry boards crackled dangerously under my feet and my eyes grew accustomed to the dark. I could just make out a pile of something at the back. I realized as I got closer it was him. He was bent over and bound in the same way I had been. I couldn't tell if he was conscious or not; he wasn't moving.

"Kyle, you're going to be okay, but we have to move fast," I said, not knowing if he heard me and unable to see him clearly in the dark. He was nothing more than a shadow before me. I knelt beside him and touched his back. He was breathing and as I ran my hands up toward his face I could feel that he was gagged. I followed the gag to the back of his head where it ended in a knot. It was too dark and the knot was too tight to undo, so I tried, unsuccessfully at first, to slip it off. Moving it up made it tighter, so I went the other way. It budged but he must have had a rag in his mouth, too, because he started to gag, so I stopped.

"I'm going to do that again," I cautioned him. "It's going to hurt, but I need to get that gag off you. Okay, here goes." I pushed it down at the back of his head. He began to gag again, but I kept going. His long hair was tangled in the gag and I could hear it pulling and tearing as I pushed on the knotted fabric. He whimpered a little before the knot slackened. I carefully removed the rag from his mouth as I could feel it sticking. He took a breath and tried to speak but he was too dry.

"We'll get you some water soon, but we have to get out of here now," I said. "They'll be back soon. I'll be right back."

I walked carefully back to the hole in the floor and the staircase. It was easier to retrace my steps, because of how the light was shining, but I still had to walk carefully, because the floorboards creaked threateningly below me. I reached the bottom of the small staircase and shouted down to Nigel whose face appeared between the treads.

"I have him, but I need a knife or some scissors." Bid poked her head in beside Nigel's and tossed up a box cutter.

"Hurry," was all she said.

I let Kyle know what I was doing, so he wouldn't fight me thinking I meant him harm. I cut the tape around his neck first, advising him to just leave the tape in place once I had cut his hands free; he had been here longer than I was a captive, so the glue on the duct tape might have bonded with his skin. I let him know that he was weak and might be unable to stand once he was free. Then, while I finished cutting the tape that bound his ankles to his wrists, he blindsided me by growling hoarsely, "Fuck off, I'm not going with you."

"What?" I was stunned. "They'll be back soon."

"That's your problem," he croaked. "You'll have to explain to them why you're taking me."

"I'm trying to get you out of here," I said pressing him. "Let's go."

"Fuck you!"

"I have your mother downstairs," I said. "I'm here with your mother, for God's sake!"

"Fuck that; you're that Robert from New York or someone with Robert's gang," he rasped. "Sal told me you were looking for me. I don't know what the fuck you want with me, but you can go to hell. I'll take my chances with Sal. All I have to tell him is who supplies me and he'll let me go," his voice trailed off in a laboured whisper.

"What?" I could not believe my ears. "No, no, you've got it all wrong. Your mother's downstairs!"

"Don't give me that bullshit. I'm staying."

I suddenly felt a strong dislike for this kid. I jumped to my feet and ran to the opening in the floor. Nigel was almost frothing at the mouth, "What the hell's taking you so long?"

"He doesn't want to go," I said. "He thinks I'm with Robert's gang and we're going to kill him if we take him."

"Oh, for Christ's sake!" said Nigel throwing up his hands.

"The little shit," said Bid, who stuck her head in. "He's going to get us all killed. Wait, I'll be back." And her head disappeared.

Tamara appeared in the crack between the stairs. "Okay, all evidence of us is gone. I'm going to start spraying the dope around, all right?"

"Right," I said. "Make it look good."

She disappeared. Bid was back looking through the space between the stairs with Karen. "He doesn't believe us," said Bid to Karen. "You'll have to convince him. He's all yours."

"Kyle?" she began quietly.

"You're going to have to shout," I said. "He's in the attic."

"Kyle!" she yelled, making me jump. From what I had heard about this kid, he was probably far more familiar with his mother's shouting voice anyway. "Kyle! Let's get out of here!"

He must have been listening from just inside the opening, because his head poked out of the hole. "Mom?" He was obviously surprised.

"I'll help you down," I said to him. "Everybody back in the van," I yelled down.

"Just in time," Tamara burst in. "Amanda says Sal is on his way back."

I had Kyle down to the second floor in good time and went to the bathroom to pull up the attic stairway. As I reached up to get a good grip on the rope, my old buddy the floating rib popped out again, making me yelp in pain. I tried to get Kyle to help, but he was as weak as a kitten.

"Nigel!" I shouted down.

"I'm here."

"Push up on the stairs and we'll pull from here."

Nigel must have taken the lion's share of the weight, because it was far easier to pull up on the rope this time, and as I lashed the rope to the cleat on the wall, my rib popped back into place again. I stopped and scooped up the bat from the main level before leaving. We flew down the stairs as fast as our legs would carry us and we crunched over some of the thousands of empty pills that now littered the floor on the way out. Kyle's eyes were like saucers looking at the pills scattered about. Then I closed the front door.

"Get into the van," I said to Kyle. He paused. "Go!" I heard Bid behind me on the phone with the 911 dispatcher, reporting screams, shots fired, and fighting at the house.

"Why did you close the door?" asked Nigel in a panic.

"I want this to look convincing," I said. "I want the cops to have no excuse to not go in." Then I wrapped my arms around my own chest to brace my tender rib, raised my right leg and planted a kick as hard as I could right on the lock. The door gave way easily, splintering the door frame where the latch was. As the door swung open, it struck the palm tree and the opaque glass shattered all over the floor. It now looked suspicious, like a forced entry.

I was just in the van, the door was still sliding closed, when Bid yelled to Amanda at the wheel, "Punch it!"

The front of the house on Baldwin was a triumph of theatrical set dressing. There were pills of every colour littering the walkway, the lawn, and inside the house throughout the hallway. Tamara had shown extra creativity by throwing them all over the two cars parked out

167

front. Morning dew had fallen on the city so the gelatin caps were sticking nicely to the cars. They looked hazardous, but of course they were empty and harmless. The front door was wide open, revealing a splintered latch and door frame, the window was smashed, and there were small holes in the back wall that resembled bullet holes. Our last view of the house as we pulled away from the curb was Burly, Skinny and Sal creeping into the foyer from the back room looking utterly bewildered. They saw our van start to pull away and ran out of the front door to get a better look.

"Shit!" I said, in a panic. "The plates: what if they see the licence plates?"

"No problem," said Tamara. "They're prop plates from an old show, and American plates, at that."

I turned around to look at the three of them as we headed down the road. They were standing in the middle of the street, fuming in our direction. They were also completely unaware of the flashing police lights coming up behind them.

We turned the corner before we could see what happened next.

Chapter 19

"Pull over," Bid commanded once we had travelled a few blocks up Spadina. "And give me that bat." I passed it forward between the seats. She removed the battery from her cellphone and then dropped the phone onto the floor at her feet and began to mash it with the end of the bat as if she were grinding corn. She took a few pieces, hopped out of the van, and dropped them into a garbage can at the side of the road. While Bid was busy with the phone, Tamara carried a screw gun to the back of the van and removed the phony rear plate to reveal the real plate underneath. She had done both the front and rear before Bid was back in the van. We pulled away again, and Bid had Amanda stop a few more times on different streets to repeat the process until all the bits of the phone had been sprinkled in garbage cans throughout the city. "It's an old prepaid phone," she said, "It's untraceable, but I'm just making sure they can't follow a trail back to us." The last thing she threw away was the battery.

"I had to make the call from the area around the house," Bid explained. "Remember that GPS chip we talked about? The 911 operators can tell the geographic area where the call was made. Even if it's an old phone and doesn't have the GPS enabled, they can identify which cell tower the call came through. It will look authentic that the call was made in that neighbourhood."

We all sat in the seats we had arrived in, except Karen who sat on the floor where she cradled her son's head as he lay beside her. As the sun began to rise over the city behind us, we drove the rest of the way back to my place in silence.

The Scotch was back out, and so was the water jug, but no one had touched the water. There was coffee brewing, too, but that was just for show. No one wanted coffee. Tamara, Nigel, and Amanda all sat on the couch with their feet up on my coffee table and their heads flopped back so they were all staring at the ceiling. Karen and Kyle were in the bathroom where I had armed them with a big bottle of alcohol and a bag of cotton balls from my makeup kit to help remove the bits of tape and glue from Kyle's neck and wrists. It sounded like the tape had stuck very well in places. Other than the occasional whispered exclamations when his mother rubbed his skin with the alcohol, Kyle hadn't said a thing. I don't know if he was shy, embarrassed, or just the shithead everyone else thought he was. I was reserving judgment; I was leaning toward shithead, though.

I stood while Bid carefully unwound the squib guard from my chest. She had already taken off my shirt. We both had to be careful not to get cut on the tiny shears that were still attached to the fabric. Their little sharp points had worked themselves into the fabric of the squib guard so they had to be removed with tweezers. My shirt, ripped and bloodstained, looked like I had worn it in a gunfight in an old Western.

She unwound the guard slowly and then removed the spent squibs and the ones that hadn't been detonated and placed them on the table. She then handed the guard to Tamara, who reluctantly dragged herself

170

up from the couch, folded the guard, and placed it back in its carrying case. Karen joined us.

"Kyle's just washing up," she said. "We used almost all of your alcohol. I'll get you some more."

"Don't worry about it," I answered. I was about to put on a clean shirt when Bid said she wanted to have another look at my chest and began to unwind the bandage. The air was cool on my skin after having been tightly wrapped for the last few hours, and my chest didn't look too bad, according to Bid. It hadn't gotten any worse, at least.

"Could it get any worse?" asked Tamara. "I thought you were going to the gym lately. . . . oh, you mean the bruising." She added a few yucks for effect. "I will say this, though," she added, "this past night was a masterpiece. We went in, created a show, and then removed all evidence of the show. I think if we had had more time, Bid would have painted the floor black." She laughed.

"Paint the floor black?" Karen asked.

"Whenever a show closes down and moves out, the last job is to paint the floor black," said Bid. "That way, the next show gets a clean slate to start their show on."

"Yours was the crowning moment though," said Nigel to Tamara. "You turned it into an art installation with those coloured pills. That was beautiful!"

"God, I only wish we could have stayed behind to see what went on afterward," said Tamara. "Do you guys do this every weekend?"

Kyle came out of the bathroom and stood beside his mother. He was gently rubbing the back of his neck. They were facing us like they were going to give us bad news. For some reason I was surprised that he was taller than his mother. Kyle had some red marks on his neck and wrists where they had scrubbed a little too hard with the alcohol and from having been bound so long.

"You're going to have to put some cream on your neck and wrists when you get home," Amanda offered. "Otherwise the alcohol will dry out your skin and it will crack." Karen nodded. They stood there for a few seconds, looking uncomfortable, like two actors who had not only forgotten their lines, but didn't know whose line it was. Actually, Karen looked uncomfortable. Kyle looked more like a mannequin, as though if he stood there long enough, he would disappear and we would all forget that this was all about-him. His mother turned toward him and stared as only a mother can, with penetrating eyes, her lips tight and thin. Anyone with a mother has been on the receiving end of a look like that. He must have felt the tension because his eyes briefly shot in her direction. He still said nothing, so Karen, clearly irritated, took the lead.

"I really cannot express how grateful I am for what you have all done today." She looked at each of us, wringing her hands. "I had no idea what kind of trouble Kyle was in and had no idea what would be involved. What you have all done is not only remarkable, it was very brave. Thank you." She shot him another look.

He seemed to feel the look, took a breath, and flatly said, "Thank you," and started to walk toward a chair to sit down.

I didn't like his tone, and I certainly didn't appreciate his brevity. I'm no one's parent, but I am in the communicating business, and that sounded like we were being short-changed. Karen seemed to be happy with it, though. I looked around the room to see what the others might be thinking and they all wore expressions of disappointment.

"Nope!" I said, surprising even myself. "Not good enough." Amanda looked at me as though I had stolen money from a church, but I turned to Karen and continued. "Karen, I accept your thanks on behalf of the rest of us." I glanced at the rest and no one objected. Then I concentrated on Kyle. "You, sir, on the other hand, owe these people more than that. You don't owe them money or even your gratitude. Gratitude is cheap goods. What you owe them is an explanation." He started to move his head, but I wasn't finished so I stopped him by holding up my hand. "We know how you got into this mess with Sal and his group. What we don't know is how this all started."

He attempted to retreat into the teenage panacea "I dunno," so I stopped him.

"Look, we're not cops and we're not stupid. Once you leave this place, we'll never see you again. We're in the story business and we know that every story has a subtext." He looked at me blankly, so I explained. "An underlying motive for actions. We want to know what made you think this was a viable career path, and how a seventeen-year-old gets his hands on enough veterinary drugs to sell not only in bars, which you are too young to get into, but speakeasies, which are even more elite."

"Veterinary drugs?" asked Karen.

"Yeah," said Nigel. "Ketamine or K or Special K. It's a veterinary drug."

"How could you?" She exploded at Kyle, rushing toward him and shouting directly in his face.

"Karen, you can't interrupt anymore. This is between Kyle and us," I said, but she didn't hear me. She flew into a rage.

"How dare you? They're my friends!" Kyle just turned away and rolled his eyes.

"Wait a minute, Michael," interrupted Bid. "Before you continue with Kyle. Karen, is there something more we need to know?"

It was a good thing she asked. We probably took a shortcut to the crux of the matter by getting some background from Karen. It turned out that Kyle wasn't doing well at school. He used to be a good student, but now his marks were low and he had behavioural issues. His parents, naturally, thought it was because he was too bright and he was bored with the curriculum. The school hinted that there were other reasons, but Karen and Rob wouldn't believe their son had psychological issues. The school suggested an adjusted program of study. So, a part of this adjusted program would be a co-op placement in a field where Kyle had an interest. Karen thought a placement in a veterinary clinic would be perfect. Kyle had always been good with animals, she said, and she had a vet friend who owned a clinic. That seemed to establish a connection between Kyle and proximity to the drug, but I wondered how he could actually get access enough to sell. Bid thanked Karen for the back story, and then told her we needed to hear the rest from Kyle.

"So, how did you get the dope from the clinic?" I asked. He just clammed up. I wanted to throttle him. "Look, tough guy," I said. "You want to play it that way? Fine, but here's how it's going to go down. You tell us now, and you get to leave here and start over. You refuse to tell us, and I go to the cops. It's as simple as that." Karen looked horrified. "I don't know you. I don't care about you, or your parents, or your parents' reputation. What I care about are the other people in this room. These people did what they did tonight for each other; Amanda wanted to help your mother, and we wanted to help Amanda. So, if you mock our benevolence with your contemptible uncooperativeness, I will go to the cops. And once the cops get their hands on you, your name will be common knowledge. You can bet that anybody you've pissed off in the past will come looking for you, and brother, they'll find you. You'll go to jail, too. And don't think you can hide in there because they'll find you there, too. And by the way, all the things you've heard that happen in prison," I paused, "they're true." He seemed to be listening, so I continued, although I had no idea what I was talking about. I had no intention of going to the police, and the only thing I knew about prison was what I had seen in the movies. I punctuated my rant by enunciating every consonant of, "How did you get the dope?"

I think it was the *what happens in prison* reference that swung him around.

Turned out, it was all very simple. He was good with computers, so he cracked the administrator's password on the vet's computer network soon after arriving at the clinic. It wasn't because he was any kind of hacker or programming wizard, he just looked over people's shoulders a few times when they were logging in and learned the password. Then he just adjusted the pharmacy orders slightly and skimmed off the overages when they arrived at the clinic. He started small, but he said he was getting braver lately because he was selling more.

"You'll quit that placement," said Amanda suddenly from the couch.

"That wasn't part of his deal!" said Kyle hotly, pointing at me.

"I'm adding a clause to the deal," said Amanda.

"That's not fair!" he said petulantly.

"Fair? Fair?" I found myself blurting out. "What would have been fair is your mother keeping the iPhone and throwing you in the lake on Friday night! People have put their necks on the line for you this weekend, boy. They've given you a chance to begin again. This is your choice. Your parents, your teachers, nobody else can do this for you. You are in charge of your future, and your life is at a crossroads right here in this room. Whatever choice you make will be yours alone." Then I hastily added, "Although I am sure your mother will have lots to say about it." Karen shot me a look.

"He's right," said Nigel dryly. "You don't even have to make the choice here in front of us. Keep it to yourself if you want to. If choosing because it's the right thing isn't enough, do it to keep out of prison.

"Okay, I'm off," groaned Nigel suddenly, pushing himself up from the couch. "I've had enough of you folks for one day, and I'm tired. Tamara, did you say you were driving us home?"

"I will if you will all help me carry this stuff back to the van, and don't forget to bring down the car seat." Nigel was up and moaning as he hefted the car seat.

Karen and Kyle were the first to leave as the others collected the gear. Karen said thank you again, and I asked her to please keep what had happened to herself. I didn't even want to think of the kind of trouble we could get into if our activities got out. She agreed and they were gone. I still didn't like Kyle. I was sure he would return to his old ways, but it really was out of our hands. I felt sorry for his parents, but not too sorry. It would be like feeling sorry for the grasshopper in the fable about the ant and the grasshopper. I was pretty sure they had made this mess by what they had done, or not done, over the past seventeen years.

Once everyone had left, I cleaned up everything, the Scotch, water, coffee; I put the furniture back to where it belonged; I threw out my ripped shirt and even emptied the bathroom garbage can where Karen and Kyle had thrown out the tape and the cotton balls from cleaning his neck and hands. I made the place look like no one had been there. I wanted to be able to wake up after sleeping with no evidence of the past twenty-four hours. Drained, I fell into bed. Before I drifted off to sleep, the cat hopped up on the bed and positioned herself near my feet. She had never done that before. True to her character though, she faced away from me, just to let me know she still held me in contempt. I fell asleep to the sound of her purring.

Chapter 20

It was around four thirty in the afternoon when I woke up. The sun was shining through my window and directly in my face. I was still exhausted but there was no way I could lay there any longer with the sun pouring in on me. The cat was gone. I showered and dressed, thinking I would reward myself with a Sunday dinner out. Some kind of comfort food was in order, although, I had no idea what I wanted to eat. I thought I would take a slow walk along Bloor Street until something caught my eye. My ribs were tender, but at least they didn't feel like a threat anymore, and as long as I didn't reach up or out too far, they would hopefully stay in place.

I was leaving to head up to Bloor when I met my neighbour, Dennis, just putting his key into the lock, having just arrived home from work.

"Oh, I have your Internet USB stick," I remembered. "Hang on, I'll get it." I ducked back into my apartment where I found it still poking out the back of the laptop. He had followed me in and noticed that when I pulled the stick out, the laptop woke up.

"A friend of yours?" he said pointing to the cached Twitter page on the screen. "Nice looking, in a greasy sort of way." It was Sal's Twitter page.

"No," I said too quickly, while slamming down the screen to let him know it was private. Dennis, however, does not subscribe to the notion of privacy. I handed him the stick.

"Well?" his eyebrows were arched high on his forehead. "In that case, I want to hear everything."

"There's really nothing to tell," I lied. "We were doing some research on a show and this was all part of it."

"Crap," he said. "There was a woman in your group last night who is not an actor. She was dressed too well, and she thanked me too genuinely. She looked like she was in trouble. Is she?"

"Look, it's all done now," I said, trying to give it some finality. He wasn't buying it. "I can't really say any more." I was hoping that would end his questioning, but Dennis was shrewd.

"All right," he began, "You can choose not to tell me, but that would be a silly and petty reason to end a friendship, choosing to show me that you don't trust me. How can I remain friends with someone that clearly feels I don't warrant his trust?" I felt this was a little over the top, but then he clinched the deal with, "It really doesn't matter anyway. Once I get this stick into my computer, I can track all you have done with it over the past few hours. Whatever websites you have visited and wherever this stick has been is logged on it." He had me. "Look," he continued like a salesman closing a sale, "You'll come in. I'll make dinner. You'll tell me what's going on, and I'll erase all that is on the stick without even looking at it. Isn't that reciprocal trust?"

"What're we having?" I asked defeated.

"Indian."

"Indian? You're going to make Indian food? That'll take all night" I said.

"I'll order in."

"I thought you were making dinner," I said warily.

"I'll serve it on my plates," he said flippantly. "Same diff. Come on in and I'll get you a beer while I phone it in."

It was actually a relief to tell him what had happened. I started out with the intention of just glossing over the events of the weekend, but as I began the story assumed the life of a snowball rolling downhill. I recounted how we tracked Kyle's friends, traced him to the rave, and then to where he was held prisoner. Dennis was duly impressed that we were able to keep our identities under wraps, and how we finally rescued the boy by outsmarting Sal and his boys. Dennis kept the beer flowing while I unloaded the story. I was careful to not divulge anyone's name, but of course he knew most of us were actors, and he would be able to discover their identities by just coming to the next show. All he would have to do is to read the program. I probably shouldn't have taken so much beer on board; I hadn't had anything to eat since the omelette at about three o'clock in the morning. But, telling a story is thirsty work and, like any actor, I drank what was offered; like any drunk, I talked more than I should. By the time the food arrived I was half in the bag and ready to devour it, which I did.

I have to give Dennis some credit here. It is not enough to be a good storyteller. There has to be a good listener for it to go well, and Dennis was a great listener. He laughed at the few funny bits, which of course weren't funny when they happened, gasped at the violence, was suitably shocked by the drugs, and appalled by Kyle's behaviour and disrespect. At the end of the meal I was well and truly contented. I was much more relaxed, full of good food and safe from the goons. I sat on Dennis's overstuffed couch and Casey and Finnegan hopped up and took a place on either side of me. It was all very snug and pleasant. He passed me a cognac.

"I really shouldn't," I said with an extra-large yawn, but then I pressed the glass to my lips. "God, I can't believe how tired I am."

"It's been a big weekend for you," he said. "It was a pity you couldn't have left a note for the cops, giving directions to the storage locker where they keep their dope."

"I thought of that," I said. "But there was no way to do it without compromising Sal and his lads getting arrested. I didn't want the cops to think it was a setup, even though it was. The thing about them," I continued, "is everyone who deals with them thinks they are a much bigger gang than they really are."

"Fair enough," he said while packing up the leftovers and putting them in the fridge. "They had the same perception of you guys. Didn't you say that Nigel gave Sal the impression he was a big shot from New York?" My eyes were getting too heavy to stay open any longer so I drained the last of the cognac in my glass, stood up, being careful of my ribs, and bid Dennis good night while I tottered on my way to the door. Casey and Finnegan escorted me, doing their little dance around my feet as I tried not to trip on them.

"Looks like these two are ready for their walk," he said. "Oh, and don't worry about the Internet stick."

"It's fine," I said. "You don't have to erase it. I've told you everything, anyway."

"Well, that's just it," he said, sheepishly. "It doesn't really log everything; I lied. I was just nosey. I tricked you into telling me."

What about all that talk about trust, I thought.

As my head touched my pillow, I glanced at the clock on my bedside table. It was only nine thirty. I was dead tired, even after having slept most of the day. I wondered how the others were doing.

That night, I slept like a baby. In other words, I tossed and turned and cried all night. I had dreams of being bound and gagged and kicked, waking up bathed in sweat with my heart pounding. I would eventually get back to sleep, only to get locked in another nightmare where I was being drowned by Amanda, while Nigel stood over me looking the other way and saying to someone unseen, "Your use of the word is incorrect; it's *currently*, not *presently*!" I probably shouldn't have had that last cognac at Dennis's place, but I have to admit the Shrimp Vindaloo and Aloo Gobi might have played a supporting role in my night terrors. I woke so many times that I was glad when the clock finally came within an hour of the alarm so I could just wait out the time to get up.

I left early for rehearsal and didn't even bother pulling out my script on the Queen Street streetcar. I just stared out the window as Monday-morning Toronto passed by. The sun shone, but the air was felt colder, and the sudden change from the Indian summer we had enjoyed over the past week was a stark reminder that winter was on its way. The pedestrians were divided into those who had heeded the weather report and worn jackets, and those who were shivering in the shorts and flip-flops they had worn the week before. Because I had left so early, I had time to kill on my way to work, so I strolled from the streetcar to the church. As I came around the corner to the front door of the church, I discovered Nigel seated on the concrete front steps with two very large coffees in a cardboard tray.

"You're here early," I said.

"Waiting for you." He handed me one of the coffees as I dropped my backpack. "The door's still locked anyway."

"How long have you been here?" I said peeling up the lid flap.

"Not long; the coffee's still hot." He looked tired. I sat down beside him on the concrete step and placed the paper cup against the side of my neck. I like to do that when it's cold. It keeps me warm.

"How did you sleep?" I asked.

182

"I didn't really," he said. "You?"

"Not even as much as that." I looked straight ahead and took a big mouthful of coffee. "This is one for the books; we're here before Bid. We'll have to mark this on the calendar."

"How are the spare ribs this morning?"

"Sore but still in the right place so far," I said. "I didn't get a chance to thank you for helping out this weekend. I am sorry for putting you through all that. It started out feeling like a game, really. You know, it seemed very make-believe and amateur-detective; I never imagined it would go as far as it did. Events sort of escalated steadily until they turned into a deadly serious ordeal."

"You couldn't possibly have known where it was going," he said quietly. "Besides that, I jumped in willingly if you remember. In the end, it all worked out. No one was hurt — except for you. And, hopefully, three thugs will end up in jail."

"At one point, I contemplated revenge," I said. "I think the crowning insult to us all though was Kyle's indifference to what had happened, and then his smug attitude afterward."

"I think his mother has her hands full," he said. "Wait until his father gets home!" He laughed. "I wonder if he even knows yet about his son's latest adventures."

"I wonder if he is even out of seclusion? Boy, would you want to have to explain what happened?"

The door thumped open behind us. "Did either of you even think to bring me a coffee?" asked Bid accusingly. "What are you doing out here?"

"The door was locked," said Nigel.

"Nah! It just sticks when the weather cools suddenly," she shot back. "The softwood door frame contracts at a different rate than the hardwood door. So, until they equalize, the door will be a bit sticky. It happens every year."

"This is my first year with the company," I said.

"You'll get used to it," she said. "Nigel should have remembered, though. Are you two going to get up and in here, or am I going to have to hold this door all day and risk dying of exposure?"

She had still beaten us in.

It was at least an hour more before anyone else showed up, and they were early for rehearsal, too. I looked up from my script later on to see that Amanda had arrived right on time, and she came in with David Pound. I had hoped she would arrive early so I could finally, nonchalantly invite her to lunch; although, oddly, I didn't feel any urgency in my desire to spend more time with her. She barely looked in my direction for the first little while, and then gave me only a cursory wave from the other side of the rehearsal hall. It was as if we hadn't spent the past weekend locked in some underworld intrigue. Amanda's ambivalence was a bit strange, I thought, until I realized she was smiling too broadly at Pound and laughing too loudly at his jokes, which were only marginally funny at best. Pound had a sense of humour that resembled his waistline — broad. That didn't seem to restrict Amanda's enjoyment however. I watched her stand very close to him and even touch his arm as she laughed. Then the penny dropped. I realized that any attention she had paid me was in pursuit of the project at hand. I think, however, what surprised me most was that I wasn't troubled over the loss.

The rehearsal began.

Tamara showed up just before lunch with armloads of costume pieces. She stopped to let me have another go at the pants she had adjusted.

"These fit perfectly," I said. "When did you have time to do these?" I was too surprised to even guess at where she had found the time.

"A few hours ago," she said. "I didn't feel like sleeping much last night."

"I didn't get time to thank you for everything," I said quietly while slipping the pants off and putting my street clothes back on. "We couldn't have done what we did without you."

"Any time," she said. And then seriously, "I mean that." Next, as if she had flipped a switch, she said, "How are the ribs? You know, I was just kidding when I made that crack about the gym last night. You don't look half bad without a shirt, really."

"Steady girl," I said. "You don't want to give me any ideas."

"Forget that," she snapped back. "You're still an actor and that's like a different species. God, you're giving me the willies! *Brrr*." Then she winked and walked away smiling.

"Ladies and gentlemen!" Bid called out to the whole hall. The room went silent. "Thank you. Tomorrow we will begin our ten-out-of-twelves. For you new members of the company, we will be working twelve-hour days for the next few days until the show opens. We'll start at ten a.m. and go until ten p.m. Tomorrow we will begin with a run-through and then start a technical rehearsal that will run until we are finished . . . or ten p.m., whichever comes first.

"Any questions? . . ." There were none. "Ladies and gentlemen — five minutes, please!" The day continued.

Chapter 21

The last week of rehearsal is the time when everything in the show is tightened up and locked down. We had moved the company from the church basement to the main stage in the theatre, and the rehearsals went smoothly. The show was going to be fantastic. The designer and the grips were working overnight like elves, building, painting, and moving in set pieces. Every day we came in to see new additions to the set and had to take care not to touch the paint still drying. It wasn't unusual to arrive in the morning to see the lighting grid lowered to eye level on the stage or over the seats in the house, the gaffers bolting and chaining lights to it. We would have to wait until all the safety chains were secured and they had winched the grid up to the ceiling again so we could work on the stage.

David Pound was still regularly giving us notes, but for the most part, they were just for fine tuning. There was nothing further about character development, just about things like staying within the audience's sightlines, or the approximate size of a spotlight where we had to stay rooted or risk disappearing into the blackness on stage. Most smart actors will find their light and know enough to stay within it while on stage so they can be seen. But the new kids and apprentices who had never worked on a big stage before needed the notes.

That week was a blur, as the last week in rehearsal always is. We spend our time committing our roles not only to cerebral memory but also assigning them to muscle memory, trying to make the actions we have contrived seem as natural as we hope the lines sound. We also have to adjust to the other actors' slight modifications to their readings and movements, because so much of good acting is actually reacting and listening. It is a collaborative art form, so dependent on co-operation and teamwork.

Actors working in a show together become so attuned to each other's intellectual processes and feelings that they begin to think alike and can easily anticipate each other's thoughts. It's no wonder so many romances begin while working on a show. That wasn't going to be my case though. It was clear to me from the dwindling interaction I was having with Amanda, and the apparent escalating interaction she was having with the director, that any chance I had at a close relationship with her was long gone.

It was now the press's turn to fall in love with Amanda. Her performance was going to be the talk of the town and her name would be on everybody's lips. In fact, interviews with the newspapers and CBC Radio were already taking place during our breaks. On her way into work one morning, she had to stop by Citytv to do an on-camera interview on the breakfast show. The day before, a camera crew had arrived at the theatre to shoot the rehearsal. So we mocked up a rehearsal for the camera by doing one of the comic scenes in our street clothes.

The cameraman, looking as though he was more accustomed to shooting sports, chased around the stage after us while we tried to keep out of his way. It was rather like trying to avoid a Labrador

Retriever when you have a pocket full of cookies. He always seemed to be too close behind me while shooting over my shoulder. I tried to tone down my movements for fear of hitting him with my flailing arms, as my character was inclined to do. He even followed me up onto a chair. As I was standing on a chair, delivering a comic oratory, I turned around and there he was, right behind me, or rather the camera was. He was holding it high above his head behind me, and as I turned, I was surprised to be nose to lens. Then he asked that we stop and start the scene again. This time, when we did the same scene, he followed Nigel around, shooting toward me over Nigel's shoulder for a few minutes. It was all very exciting for those few minutes; then we were sent to the dressing rooms to change into costume and makeup for our dress rehearsal. I lingered for a while by the curtain, watching as the cameraman shot Amanda while she was in a quiet discussion with Pound the director, which they concluded with large laughs at some unspoken joke.

"That's our button," said the camera man. "We'll use that piece to close the segment. It looks great. I'll cut it this afternoon and it will be on the breakfast show tomorrow when Barbara interviews you."

I had set my VCR to tape the breakfast show the next morning, since I knew I would be fast asleep when it aired. On opening night my ritual is to sleep in. Like most actors, I have many rituals not only for opening night, but also for every night at the theatre. There are things you cannot say and things you cannot do in the dressing room or on the stage, which are theatrical customs and superstitions, but there are little things I have created for myself to do to get ready at the theatre.

Opening night means no rehearsal that day, unless the play is a disaster or some calamity occurs, like a change in the script, someone gets injured or worse. None of that applied to our show, so the day was mine. I always get up late on opening day and take my time to enjoy a full breakfast. I spend the day alone, getting my clothes ready for the evening and buying opening night gifts and cards for the cast and crew. This morning, I got breakfast ready and sat down to eat while I watched Amanda's interview. I sat at my table behind a perfect omelette, grilled tomato, coffee, juice, and the TV remote control. The cat sat on the chair beside mine, purring, but as usual, with her back to me. She was obviously trying to make a point about how she was actively holding me in contempt; the purring only meant she enjoyed it.

I pushed the play button on the VCR. There was a long segment where the interviewer asked Amanda questions about her life, her career, and the show. Her answers were charming and animated. Although she was primarily a stage actor, she had a face and presence made for the camera. She was gracious and elegant without looking forced or pretentious, and her easygoing style paired nicely with her warm honey-toned voice. And, of course, she looked fabulous. While she talked about the show they played the tape that was shot the day before. Yesterday's cameraman had truly known what he was doing. He had shot over our shoulders and then pieced it all together to follow the conversation that was taking place on the screen. Because it was a piece rehearsed for the stage and had to be played very large so that the intention of the scene could be read from the last seat in the back row, it looked a bit over the top for TV but surprisingly good. I was glad I had toned down my arm movements for the camera. As I read my last line of the scene, from high atop the chair, the camera cut to Amanda and Pound laughing at that unsaid joke, making it look as though it was me who had said something hilarious. It couldn't have gone better for me. I would save this tape.

189

Later on that day, with my arms full of bags of small gifts, I hailed a cab and dashed to the theatre for opening night. I left the cab and entered through the stage door at the side of the theatre. I could not have been more pleased with myself. I had a full belly, tonight was opening night, and I was a working actor. Life was good.

I showed my pass to the guard who was playing cribbage at the security desk with one of the crew members. He waved me in and I headed for the dressing rooms to place the gifts and cards at each person's spot on the makeup tables. I was the first one there. Technically my call wasn't until a half-hour before the curtain went up, but I always like to be at the theatre at least two hours early. That way I can relax, forget about any distractions, and settle in to the work I have to do later; it's all about concentration and focus for me.

As the others began to trickle into the dressing rooms, the noise level and excitement began to increase. We all try to pretend that opening night is like any other day, but it most certainly is not. The length and success of the run of the show will depend on the reviews written about the opening night performance, and we have to deliver.

The secret is to contain your excitement and keep the flow of adrenaline from having your energy level peak too early. What you want is a steady release over the course of the evening.

I sat down at my mirror to begin my makeup. I carefully laid out the colours I would use and began to apply my character's face.

The audience was on its feet at the end of our opening-night show. Once all the well-wishers had left the green room and the dressing rooms, and we had finished celebrating the opening, we went to an all-night deli on Queen Street for something to eat. Nothing sharpens the appetite like an opening-night success. We knew the show had gone well, but the papers would tell us how well. The whole company showed up at the deli, with the actors arriving first and the crew arriving a little later, once they had reset the stage for the next day. The last to arrive were Amanda and David Pound who sat with Nigel far across the room from me. We waited there for the first newspapers to hit the stands. A group of newspaper boxes sat just outside the deli's front door, and we positioned ourselves as close to the big front window as possible, to make sure we saw when the delivery truck arrived, which it did at around two o'clock. I think we took the delivery man by surprise. As he leapt off the back of the truck with two bundles of papers, we began to applaud from inside the deli. The man thought we were mocking him, and promptly returned our greeting by giving us the finger. The driver, who had joined him to get the papers into the box, quickly said something to him while indicating us, and the assistant nodded with his mouth open. The driver had experienced this before. It was a tradition of this theatre company to wait in the deli for the first reviews and applaud the paper as it arrives. Once the papers were in the box, the driver gave us a wave through the window. The assistant gave us an uneasy smile and a small hand-flick of a wave and then jumped on the back of the truck to get to the next box down the street.

One of the company's junior members scrambled outside to get the first paper and returned handing it to Nigel, who stood to read it aloud.

"May I?" asked Nigel formally to the whole company, with his arms spread wide. He then proceeded, in his roundest tones, to read the review. He began cautiously but got bolder and increasingly dramatic as he continued through what was a perfect review. He would pause after he had read someone's name and offer them a small bow, to which the group responded with applause. I was named briefly with Nigel, and we bowed across the restaurant toward each other — a great ending to a great night.

I wearily laboured up the stairs to my second-floor apartment. I had stayed out far later than I intended to. I tried to keep my apartment keys from jingling as I pulled them out of my pocket. I leaned against the archway of the blind corner at the top of the stairs to sort my keys. I was facing Dennis' door, with my door at my left. To the right there is a hallway that runs from my door, past Dennis' and out to the back fire escape. I couldn't see down to the fire escape; not only because of the archway that obstructed my view, but the light bulb had obviously burnt out since last night. A darkened hallway and a suddenly burnt-out bulb in the middle of the night might be enough to raise many people's suspicions, but I was flying too high after our performance and the early reviews in the paper. I should have at least glanced down the hall before sliding my key into the lock. I was too preoccupied with the newspaper tucked under my arm and steadying myself after the few B & Bs I had poured down the back of my throat. The all-night deli wasn't licensed for liquor, but Nigel had brought a paper bag with Benedictine and Brandy that we had passed around and poured into coffee cups while we digested the reviews.

I turned the key and opened my door.

"Good evening," came a low voice from behind me. It wasn't threatening, but my hair stood on end nonetheless. I turned toward the voice and dropped the newspaper to free my hands. I had already had enough of people sneaking up on me to last a lifetime. With my foot, I quickly swept the newspaper behind me and into my apartment, so I wouldn't trip over it if I had to move forward in a hurry. Then I stood in a power position, something they teach you in theatre school that gives you the look of control. You stand at a forty-five degree angle to your opponent, with your feet shoulder width apart and your hands hanging loose at your sides. I admit, the posture also helped keep me from swaying. The man in the shadows had been silent for a few seconds, but now he stepped forward one pace and unhurriedly reached high over his head to tighten the curly fluorescent light bulb. He kept his gaze on me while he screwed it back in, and the light buzzed then blazed to life, revealing him to me. I had never seen him before. He was tall and even under his jacket I could see he was powerfully built. The bright light cast severe shadows, making him squint and giving his face a dangerous quality. The most striking thing about him, though, was that he didn't have a hair on his head. Not only was he bald, but as he stepped into the light I could see that he had not even a suggestion of where a five o'clock shadow, no eyebrows or eye lashes. His skin was so smooth it shone.

"I hope I didn't scare you," he said softly and slowly. "I just turned off the light so I wouldn't frighten anyone else who might come up the stairs."

I didn't want to appear alarmed and in my fuddled state asked, "Are you a swimmer?" That clearly surprised him and he took a step back and smiled.

"No," he was trying not to laugh. He was far too calm for my liking. He wasn't worried about me at all. "I'd like to talk to you about some friends of yours: friends of ours, really."

"I don't think we have any friends in common," I said. I hadn't moved but the adrenaline was clearing my head. I wanted him out of here, but the hallway by the door was narrow, and in order for him to get by me, he would end up dangerously close in this confined space. I was trying to figure out how he got in here, too. He should have needed a key for the door downstairs. "Why don't you just turn around and walk toward the back end of this hallway." I was speaking slowly and precisely, trying to sound passively threatening and sober. "There's a door there and a fire escape. You have made a mistake and you should leave now, before you make another one."

"We've got to talk first," he said.

"Look, if you don't start to leave now, I am going to pound on my neighbour's door," I threatened. "He'll be out here in a moment and your welcome will have ended." That would convince him.

"He's at work and won't be home until this afternoon," he said confidently and then pulled his sleeve up to look at his watch. "Just about the time you leave for work again." His arms were hairless too. "Can we go inside? This will be much more pleasant if we can sit down. I've been on my feet all night waiting for you."

"I'm not having you inside. I don't even know you," I said. "I don't know anything about you. Why would I invite you into my apartment? You're certainly not a cop. You look too much like a cop to be a cop, and your shoes are all wrong." I was drawing from Megan's wisdom, I was in such a state, and trying to buy some time while I decided what my next move would be.

"Look, Michael, this won't take long." God! He knew my name! "I only want some information and then I'll be on my way."

He was clearly not leaving. Then I remembered I still had that baseball bat inside, by the couch. If push came to shove, I would at least have a weapon. So, I invited him in, or rather, I accepted his invitation to invite him in.

It was stupid of me really, to assume that I could wield a weapon against this man. As he passed by me, I realized he was not just big, but also very fit. He had the lean look and chiselled jaw of a hockey player. He moved smoothly, like a cat, and he hardly made a sound as he entered my apartment. He walked right to the centre of the living room and looked around.

"Nice place," he said. "You been living alone for a while?"

"There's a cat," I said.

"You hate your cat," he said, letting me know I had no secrets.

194

"She's not my cat."

"Have it your way." He sat down on the couch. He sat back into the corner and crossed his legs which were stretched out ahead of him. He was wearing jeans. His jeans looked new or they had been commercially cleaned and pressed. His dark brown casual leather shoes had a heavy tread like Docs. He was making himself comfortable; he wasn't going anywhere in a hurry. "I'm Frank, by the way."

"Michael Dion," I answered.

"Yes," he said, letting me know this was not news. He very nicely waved me to sit down, as if he were the host of a talk show. That was the idea, I suppose. He was going to ask me questions and I was going to answer. I looked over at him, trying not to panic. If he just reached over the arm of the couch, he would easily feel the baseball bat on the floor. He must have seen me glance at it, so he looked over the arm of the couch and picked up the bat. He turned it over in his hands and said, "This is pretty small for you. It's a child's bat."

"It's a souvenir."

"From last week? That must have hurt." He put it down again. I felt like he was teasing me.

"Okay," I said standing up. I'd had enough. "What's this about?"

"Like I said, I want to talk about some friends of ours." The muscles in his forehead flexed to form wrinkles just above where his eyebrows would have been raised. "Tell me about your relationship with Sal Bodinov."

"Who?"

"Come on," he said, while he gave me a disapproving look. "Let's be adult about this."

"Why do you want to know?" I needed to understand where this was going. If this guy was an associate of Sal's looking for revenge, this was going to get scary. He must have sensed my agitation because he leaned forward on the couch and clasped his hands in front of himself.

"I have no connection with Bodinov," he said. "I just have an interest in him. I have been watching him for a while, and trying to get him to implicate himself, but he has been too slippery for us. Not because he's intelligent, he's just lucky, I think."

"What do you mean *us*?" I asked. This conversation was starting to change direction on me. He leaned back to reach into his jacket. As he did, I noticed a shoulder holster and a gun. I stiffened a bit, until his hand reappeared holding a police badge in a wallet.

"You're a cop? Why didn't you say so?"

"Because officially, I am not here," he said. "We arrested Bodinov last week. Early one morning, we got a call from a concerned citizen that there were suspicious noises coming from a house on Baldwin Street: screams, gunshots, things that would get our attention, you know. Strangely, when we arrived at the scene, we found Bodinov and his associates standing in the middle of the street. They were surprised to see us, and we found all sorts of incriminating evidence that persuaded us to enter his house. Would you be surprised to know that we found quite a quantity of drugs in the house?" I sat dumbfounded, so he continued. "We found an assortment of empty pills, too, that had been scattered around. We discovered later they were harmless, but we certainly took notice. There was evidence of a forced entry, too. There were curious little holes in the walls and some red spatters that initially looked like blood. Turns out it was stage blood." He stopped for a moment to look me in the eye and then said, "Any time you care to jump in, feel free."

I was trying to find a way not to lie to him. I've noticed from watching police TV shows it's never good to lie to the cops, so I just skirted around the issue, hoping he would let me know how I was going to be affected. The only thing I could think was, I cannot get arrested — I'm in a show! So I said, "What brings you to tell me any of this?"

"I need some additional information," he said.

"You seem to be telling a great story so far," I offered, "and you said you had arrested this Choobookov and his two friends."

"Bodinov," he said back at me. "Nice try — and I never said there were two of them."

"Lucky guess?"

"Look, I don't have to ask you questions here," he said, leaning forward again. "We can go over to 52 Division and talk there, but this is much more informal and need not go any further."

"You know," I said, "I've recently used that very tactic on someone."

"I know. But you're not a copper. I am. And I can, and I will, make good on my promise to bring you in." He sat back again, laying his splayed arms along the back of the couch, which opened his jacket and revealed the butt of his gun. "There were a number of fingerprints in that house that we can't identify, but as soon as we get to the station and ink your digits, I have a feeling things will become much clearer to us. Not only that, but then Bodinov will know who you are and he may come looking for you, eventually. If it gets out that you're an actor, well, your career will be over, whether it's because he'll find you, and end it for you, or you have to keep yourself under wraps to hide from him and his friends. Even a best-case scenario is you'll have to confine yourself to voice-over work or radio commercials. Is there a lot of money in that?"

"Okay," I said, defeated. "Okay. What do you need to know?"

"First, I want the location of the storage unit where he keeps the rest of his dope."

At that I was suspicious, wondering if he was a dirty cop, looking to make some extra money selling the unclaimed dope, but I was in no position to question him. I wasn't ever actually at the storage place. Nigel only told me where it was, but I didn't tell Frank the cop that. I knew the general location of the place, the cross streets, not the locker number of the unit, so that was all I could give him.

"It's somewhere near Cherry Street and Lakeshore. I didn't go into the storage place. Bodinov went in alone," I said, sticking to the facts. There were probably hundreds of lockers there. It would be close to impossible to find the dope, anyway. He seemed to know where it was, nodding when I mentioned the cross streets. He didn't explain how he was going to make a legal connection between Sal and the locker, but he seemed to be happy with my answer.

"We're going to let the dogs find it for us," was how he explained it. That made him sound legit to me.

"Wait a minute," I said. "You seem to know a lot about my involvement with Bodinov. Was he under surveillance? Were we caught on camera or something?"

"No," he said. "Someone let me know that you were involved a few days afterward."

"Who?" Had someone from our group let it out of the bag? I couldn't imagine who would have. I presumed it was Karen.

"I guess it's only fair that you know who put the finger on you," he said standing up. Then, to my surprise, he walked right by me and out of my apartment. I heard a soft knock on a door, so I stood up and followed him, through my front doorway, only to meet him on his way back in with Dennis.

"What the heck are you doing here?" I asked. "He said you were at work."

"He lied," said Dennis looking guilty. "It's my day off."

"Sometimes we have to lie to get to the truth," said the cop. "I'm a friend of Dennis's. We've been friends for a long time. A few days ago, I casually told him about an arrest we had made last week. I was speaking in general terms, though; I didn't give any real details. I was just letting him know we had picked up a few guys that were really, you know, handed to us, and how odd it was. Dennis got the strangest look on his face."

"Frank here let Bodinov's last name slip, and I must have looked shocked," Dennis jumped in, "because Frank asked me if there was something wrong."

"I didn't really let anything slip," said Frank. "Bodinov's name was in the newspaper anyway, but you should have seen Dennis's face," Frank laughed. "He looked like someone had poked him with a stick. His eyes went wide like saucers. So I asked him what was the matter and Dennis said, 'Sal Bodinov?' I hadn't said Sal, so I had to find out what he knew about the case."

"I remembered seeing the name Sal Bodinov on your computer when you gave me back my USB stick," said Dennis to me. "He was the shady-looking guy on the Twitter page. Remember? When I mentioned him, you swung the laptop lid down, but the name stuck with me because I remember thinking when I saw it, 'Is that Boris's brother?'"

"Boris?" I asked.

"An old cartoon character," said Dennis. "Never mind that. The stuff you told me last week fit with the story Frank told me."

"So," continued Frank, "Dennis gave me a few details that he would have known only if he had been there, or if someone who had been there had told him. I just told him to keep going, and the version he gave me filled in all the blanks. You guys were very creative, very inventive."

"Well, you know, necessity being the mother of all that," I said, feeling betrayed. "So, are you going to cuff me and take me in?"

"You watch too much TV," said Frank. "You actually did us a favour. We had put it down to a rival gang trying to get rid of them, only the job was far too thorough for a rival gang. Mostly, if a gang wants to shut down another gang's operation, they just phone it in from a prepaid cell phone, saying something about gunshots or screams. When we get there, usually the place is either empty or we find some poor idiot in a basement tending the plants of a grow-op. We usually end up with one arrest, a house full of pot to destroy, and an embarrassed landlord who knows nothing about it, thinking he's rented the place out to a family."

"So, now what?" I asked. "What do you want me to do? Do I have to testify or something?"

"Oh, hell no," said Frank. "The official explanation is a rival gang; we're going to leave it at that. Adding you to the mix would be impossible to explain, and you can bet their lawyer will scream something about entrapment. Even Bodinov thinks you guys were another gang from New York. He keeps talking about the bikers, too. But we can't figure out which bikers he's talking about, and he's a bit vague about it himself. He's a small timer with big ideas. We just want to stop him before he gets any bigger and starts a war in the streets. No, you are done with this. You and I will probably never see each other again."

"What?" said Dennis. "That's a bit final. I do live next door to Michael you know. You are bound to bump into him once in a while, unless this is you giving me the elbow."

"No, no, of course not," said Frank, while the light bulb switched on in my head.

"Oh! You two are friends," I said. "Friends, ahh."

"We've known each other for years," said Dennis, "but now, we're getting better acquainted. It's early in this stage of the relationship, but . . ."

"Nuff said," I cut him off holding my hands up.

"Okay, it's my turn again," said Frank leaning forward, a bit relieved that I had stopped Dennis. "Why did you ask me if I was a swimmer before?"

"Oh, sorry," I said. "Actors' minds work very quickly, and I was in a bit of a panic with you standing there in the hallway looking like you might attack and kill me, and I had had a few drinks. I wanted to distract you while I thought of some way to escape."

"That doesn't make it any clearer," said Frank.

"A long time ago, I had a friend who was a swimmer, training for the Olympics, a very serious competitor. When there was an especially important swim meet, the serious swimmers used to get together the night before and shave their entire bodies. They said it made them slipperier in the water. I noticed that you had no hair at all on your head; it just triggered that memory so I blurted it out. I noticed your arm was bare too."

"Ah, I see," he said smiling and throwing his head back. "I have alopecia. It's a condition that makes me lose all my hair. It may be temporary . . . or not." He leaned his head to the side as if to acquiesce to what might be inevitable. "It's not contagious. But, I am not a swimmer," he laughed. "Well, you have a show later on today, I'll bet." He stood up. "You'll want to get to sleep."

He was right, I was exhausted and there was a show that night. Thank God there wasn't a matinee. I showed them out and stood with

201

my ear to the door listening to a few indecipherable murmurs and then footsteps down the stairs. Finally, I heard the building's front door slam below. As I walked into my bedroom I noticed the sky outside my window was beginning to lighten. It was dawn and I was going to bed; I was living the show business cliché.

I pulled the blind down and climbed under the covers. The cat jumped up on the foot of the bed and faced away from me. This was becoming a pattern. I finally went to sleep to the sound of her purring.

Chapter 22

The first Saturday night of the show's run had come and gone. The day had been full, with the afternoon matinee and the evening show. I was tired. Sunday morning would have to slip by without me. I would not wake up until after noon and then repeat the process on Monday, which was dark at the theatre. I declined the invitation to go out for drinks. I wanted to get back to my old routine that kept the self-abuse to a minimum. Late nights and too much liquor will eventually show up in an actor's work, and I didn't want that. I enjoyed working with this company, and I wanted to go on working for them in the coming years.

I noticed that the light in the hallway was out again, this time legitimately though. The bulb had broken. As I turned the corner toward my door, I felt the crackle of broken glass under my shoes. I glanced down the hallway into the darkness, first suspiciously, and then chuckling to myself at my nervousness. There were no strangers hiding down there tonight. I slipped my key into my lock and thought, *How did that light bulb break?* I must have paused to consider it, when the crunching of glass under foot from far down the hall behind me made the hair on the back of my neck rise. I twisted around and peering deep into the darkness, I watched a figure emerge. It was Kyle. He slowly walked forward a few steps and stopped.

"You scared the hell out of me," I said, relieved and smiling, wondering what he was doing here. He wasn't smiling. He was afraid. His eyes shot from side to side and then he looked over his shoulder. He lurched forward two steps, as if he had been pushed from behind. Then he rocked forward another step, and a face came into view behind him.

"I'm sorry," said Kyle in a voice thick with fear.

"Shut up!" barked the stranger behind him. Then to me, "You Dion?"

"That's right," I replied cautiously.

"You done good kid," he said to Kyle. "Okay, I don't want to see your face again, anywhere, or you're dead. Now fuck off!"

Kyle looked at me again as he passed me on his way to the stairs. "I'm sorry," he whispered again on his way by. He looked back over his shoulder at the man behind him. The stranger jolted and flapped his arms like a schoolyard bully to hasten Kyle's departure. Kyle jumped and turned to run. I watched his back as he flew toward the wooden stairs and rumbled down them. Once the door slammed below, I turned back toward the stranger and was shocked to see he had a gun pointed at me.

"Surprise!" he said quietly, waving it at me. "Don't do anything stupid, or I'll nail you where you stand." He wasn't very tall, shorter than me. He was dead serious and dangerous. Probably in his thirties and built like a fire hydrant, he was stocky and solid. His hair was too long and wild looking, and his grey-streaked chin-puff beard needed a trim. He wore a black leather jacket with too many zippers to be practical, and his jeans, although clean, were frayed at the bottoms, around the heels of his boots. He had every intention of carrying out his promise. His gun was real and I was scared to death.

"What do you want?" I asked, struggling to sound reasonable.

"Now we're on the right track," he smiled, revealing teeth that hadn't been adequately cared for. "Let's get straight to the point. Bodinov's not going to need his dope in jail. I want it. Where's his stash?"

"It's on Baldwin," I said, shaking now, but relieved that I had an answer.

"Not the house," he snarled. "Where does he hide the bulk of his dope?" He meant the locker.

"I think he keeps it in a storage place around Lakeshore," I said.

"Take me there."

"I've never been there," I quickly pointed out. "I don't know where it is. I've only heard about it."

"The kid told me you know the place."

"He was wrong," I said apologetically.

"Let's go." He waved the gun threateningly to urge me forward. I had no choice. I started to walk down the stairs ahead of him, wondering what I had gotten myself into, and cursing Kyle for bringing this guy to my apartment. At the bottom of the stairs, I reached for the doorknob and turned to look at my abductor to try to reason with him.

"I told you, I don't know where this place is," I began shakily. "Someone else told me about it, but I've never been there."

"Let's go," was all he said. Over his shoulder, way down the hallway, I noticed a small movement at the far corner. There it was again. It was Kyle, peeking around the corner. He must have slammed the door to make us think he had left, but he had hidden here. I turned again and opened the door. We both headed outside into the cool night air. I stopped at the sidewalk and turned around to see that the gun was gone and his hands were in his jacket pockets. He looked both ways to scan the street and with his head indicated a small silver car at the curb.

"Get in." I approached the passenger side but he had other ideas. "You're driving." He slipped into the back seat, right behind me, and threw the keys over my shoulder and onto the dashboard. "Let's go." After I had started the car and reached for the stick to put it in drive, he grabbed a handful of my hair from behind, wrenching my head around the headrest and pulling my hand off the wheel. "No fucking around," he said, putting the muzzle of the gun against my cheek, "or I'll plant one right into the back of your head." There was no way I was going to fuck around. I was going to do exactly what he wanted.

I had only a vague idea where I was going from what Nigel had said. He had given me the cross streets, but in Toronto, the cross streets just identify the general area where something is. Consequently, I drove around the east end of the waterfront for a while, as my friend in the back seat was getting more agitated with each wrong turn. By sheer chance, I came upon what I hoped was the right place. It was a brightly lit lot, with rows of long, one-storey buildings, fronted with green garage doors. The traffic was heavy on that street, even at this time of night. There must have been a rail yard nearby or a ship unloading on the waterfront, because there was an endless stream of large cargo trucks, loaded with ships' containers, racing by in both directions. I tried waiting for a break in the traffic to make the left turn into the driveway of the storage place. There was no break, so I stomped on the gas pedal and just made it between two trucks, the latter of which leaned on his horn to punctuate my recklessness. I rapidly slowed as soon as I was safely in the driveway, and came to a stop halt with the nose of the car pointed at a closed, four metre, chain-link gate.

Now what? As if in answer to my unspoken question, an old pickup truck carefully nosed around a corner inside the yard, loaded high with furniture, and pulling a small trailer, equally laden. The pickup stopped on the other side of the gate. The passenger jumped out and ran to a box on a pole, where he inserted a key. The gate shuddered and began to slowly slide open. My friend in the back seat rolled down his window and waved the truck out. As the pickup came alongside, I reluctantly gave a small wave, and my passenger also waved but masked his face with his hand.

"Go!" he said, once the pickup was behind us, so I scooted through the gate. When we were on the other side of the fence, he jumped out and pulled a ring of keys from his pocket, waving them to the pickup truck. "I've got it!" He shouted toward the pickup in a friendly way, meaning he would shut the gate. The driver of the pickup stuck his arm out of the cab and gave a grateful wave as he pulled into the street, causing one of the transports to brake suddenly. His horn blared and a smoky blue cloud rose around the rear tires as they locked up. The pickup driver never even touched his brakes. He just gently made the turn and pulled his trailer into the eastbound lane.

"All right," said my captor. "Which locker is it?"

"I don't know," I said tentatively. "I don't even know if this is the right place."

"Let's go," he said, taunting me. He must have thought I was bluffing, because he pushed me along with the point of his gun. "Enough bullshit. Just show me the locker and you can get lost."

I was trying to think. How could I possibly get away from this guy? If I just ran, he would shoot me. How good a shot was he? I needed time to think. My brain started racing. I remembered Nigel's description of the storage place from the night he came here. He said he didn't go in, only Sal did, so Nigel didn't see which locker it was. If this was the right place, and we were currently parked in the same spot Nigel had been when he was with Sal, then the locker we were looking for could not be any of those that we could see. It would have to be down one of the middle aisles. Even though I didn't know which locker it was, if I got desperate I could make a run for it. I would have a better chance if I could try to escape around a few corners, before making a break for the outside. There was a maze of corners down the middle aisles. I decided I was desperate.

"I can't remember the number," I said turning to face him. "It's down one of the middle aisles. I'll try to recognize it as we walk through."

"Now you're finally acting smart," he sneered.

The storage lot was much bigger than it looked from the street. There were many rows of buildings with different sized doors. I decided to stay in the rows with the bigger doors because I remembered that Nigel said the shipment Sal had hijacked was in a large truck, so the load would have been large. The gunman was staying close behind me as I walked down the rows. I stopped once to scrutinize a door, and then shook my head. I wanted to convince him that I was really working at this. He stayed behind a few moments after I did that, so I thought I would try it again, but closer to a corner. If he stayed behind the next time, I could duck around a corner and start to run, zigzagging through the buildings so he couldn't get a clear shot at me until I could double back and escape through the front gate. I knew it would only be a temporary escape — he knew where I lived. I would have to worry about that later.

That was my plan. As lean and provisional as it was, it was the only one I had. I stopped at a door about three from the end of the row, closest to the yard entrance. I put my hands on it, God knows why, and again shook my head. I moved on, quickening my pace, and my captor stayed behind to double-check my rejection of the door. My adrenaline kicked in and I was just about to take the last three steps before ducking around the corner, when a sound froze my insides. It was something I had only heard in the movies, but the metal against metal ratchet sound was unmistakable. It was a gun, cocking and loading. Then, from across the aisle, another one.

"Don't move," a measured metallic voice announced over a megaphone. "Lay your gun down and place your hands on the back of your head."

I placed my back against the building and slowly put my hands on my head. My captor raced to the building on the other side of the aisle, facing me. He placed his back into one of the recesses of the doors, giving him an additional eight centimetres of shelter. He was frantic, looking from side to side, but he had no intention of surrendering. Out of the corner of my eye, I caught some movement from the other end of the aisle. It was something small, shiny and round, a flash of light . . . it was a mirror coming around a corner. Instinctively, I looked over at it. My gunman saw me look in that direction and acted automatically. He squeezed off a few shots in that direction. The shots went wild, one hitting the pavement and one a garage door on the other side of the aisle. Two loud shots were returned in our direction, and I scurried around the corner and lay down on the ground by the perimeter fence. Another three or four shots came from the other end.

"Blue Team! Blue Team! Go! Go! Go!" yelled the voice on the megaphone.

The gunman wasted no time, he leapt to his feet and began running for the exit, shooting back over his shoulder. He wasn't going to let them outflank him. I stayed on the ground to let the cops catch up with him. I didn't want them to make a mistake and take a shot at me.

"He's heading for the exit!" yelled the cop on the megaphone. More shots. The gunman's boots were not meant for running. He slid sideways when he tried to make the sharp right turn at the gate and went down with a crash. He leapt up again and sprinted for the car. He flung the car door open and swung himself inside, keeping his head low to avoid being hit by a bullet. From the base of the fence, I had a clear view of him in the car as he started the engine, slammed it into gear, and spun his wheels in reverse. He hurtled backwards through the gate and away from the police. I couldn't see the police anywhere; they must have been on the other side of the row of buildings. The gunman was well ahead of them though. He hadn't even closed his door yet when he reached the end of the driveway at full speed. He was going to get away.

It could not have been timed any better . . . or worse. The traffic hadn't abated since we had arrived a few minutes before. The transport trucks were still flying by in both directions. If he had been a second later, the eastbound truck would have missed him, or at worst, clipped the trunk of his car as it entered the street. It would have spun the car and damaged it, and he might have been injured, but he may have been able to escape on foot. That wasn't the case, though. Instead, I watched in horror as he reached the centre of the street at high speed, where, simultaneously, an eastbound truck caught the front of his car and the westbound truck hit the back of the car. The dual impact spun the car a quarter revolution between them, and the car disappeared momentarily from my view as the heavy container trucks crushed it between them like a mosquito between two hands. Both trucks stopped in a shriek of brakes and clouds of blue smoke on either side of the car, which was now just a flattened mass of tangled sheet metal and automotive fluids.

I stood up, breathless, waiting for the police to appear so I could explain. I put my hands on my head. I was still standing that way when they surprised me from behind.

"Are you okay?"

I turned around slowly expecting the barrel of a rifle in my face, but there stood Bid and Nigel, with their hands full of office supplies: a clipboard each and staplers. Bid had a dental mirror peeking out of her pocket. I don't know how you are supposed to respond in a situation like that, but I swear I thought I was dreaming. I nodded dumbly that I was fine, as my knees began to buckle. Nigel steadied me.

"Let's get out of here," Nigel said urgently, before I had a chance to say anything at all. I couldn't figure out where the police had gone. We headed for the exit and Nigel scooped up a megaphone as we passed the corner of the building. We quickly walked through the open gate, unimpeded and unnoticed. The few people who were gathered on the street were focused on the commotion in the middle of the road and the standing wreckage of the car. Traffic had stopped and drivers were getting out of their vehicles to look at the crushed car. I heard a siren in the distance and saw the lights of an ambulance far down the street as it inched its way around the stopped trucks and over the sidewalk toward the accident.

"Keep going," said Bid, handing her office supplies to Nigel. "I'll be right back." Off she ran toward the crowd. Nigel kept me walking down the street that was perpendicular to the road with the accident. We soon found his parked car. Before we could get in, Bid was back and out of breath.

"You're okay," she said. "He'll never bother you again. He's dead."

"What about the police?" I asked weakly.

"There are no police," said Bid. "We're the police. Get in the car."

"I'm letting Amanda know that all is well," said Nigel. He had his phone out and was texting. Then he pocketed his phone and suggested that we slip away from here first, before the real police arrived, and explain later.

Nigel drove up to Bloor Street and parked in plain view near Bathurst. We sat with the windows up, while crowds of people breezed by us on the sidewalk.

"How did you know I was in trouble?" I asked from the back seat. Nigel and Bid had spun inward to talk to me from the front.

"Kyle," said Bid. "He was hiding in the hallway when you were taken away."

"I saw him there," I remembered.

"He called his mother as soon as you drove away from your place," continued Bid. "Karen then phoned Amanda, and she phoned Nigel. Nigel phoned me."

"Kyle heard where you were going," broke in Nigel. "I'd been there before, so I knew where to go, but I knew I would need Bid's help. We tried to get there as soon as possible. Even though you had a good head start on us, we arrived just after you did. What took you so long to get there?"

"I didn't know exactly where the place was," I said. "I just drove around until I found it. That took time."

"We saw the gate open and you drive in," continued Nigel. "We snuck in through the gate when you both went around a corner. Then we watched for an opportunity to try to scare him off. We didn't want to corner him and force him to hurt someone, so we worked our way to the far end of the yard to give him an escape route."

"I saw you pick up the megaphone on our way out," I said, "but I heard guns."

Bid held up a large old stapler and slowly squeezed it in the air. That was the ratchet sound of a gun loading. Then she held up the clipboard with a wooden back and snapped the clip a few times. The sound was sharp and filled the car like a gunshot.

"I had a few old slices of copper pipe that I dropped on the ground every time I snapped the clipboard," said Bid proudly. "The sound rings like spent cartridges ejecting from a gun. The echo in that yard between the buildings was perfect for the sound effects." She started to smile, but stopped as she looked at me. I must have appeared frightened.

"And he's dead?" I wanted confirmation.

"Yes," said Bid seriously.

"Who was he?" I wanted to know.

"Kyle said he was someone that Sal had pissed off," explained Nigel. "He was a one-man operation. Originally, this guy was selling dope to the rave crowd. When Sal came along with a bigger supply, lower prices, and better profit for the rave owners, this guy was told to take a hike. Everyone thought Sal's gang was bigger, and this guy was on his own, so he backed off. When he found out that Sal was out of commission, he decided to go back into business and as a bonus, take control of Sal's supply."

"Where did you find this out?" I asked.

"Kyle," said Nigel. "For some reason, Kyle went nosing around the house on Baldwin yesterday and this guy just happened to be there, too. He thought Kyle was a member of Sal's gang and tried to get the info on where the stash was. Kyle was trapped, so he led him to you. He had no choice; the guy had a gun."

"So he was on his own?" I asked, hoping I had heard right.

"Correct," said Nigel.

"And he is dead?" I asked again, needing to hear it once more.

"I saw him," said Bid. "There is no doubt."

They drove me home. Before I left the car, Nigel turned around to face me in the back. His look was grim.

"Michael, I like you, and I like working with you," he began, "but I cannot continue to drag your ass out of the fire, unless you buy me that bottle of Grey Goose I was promised." He held up a hand. "There is nothing more to discuss. That is my final word on it."

"I'll have it for you tomorrow," I said. Nigel roared with laughter.

I went upstairs to my apartment and replaced the bulb in the hallway right away. Then I got a broom and swept up the broken glass from the hallway floor all the way down to the rear fire escape door. I paused a few times to listen for suspicious noises. Then, with the broom tightly held in my hands, I checked the lock on the fire escape. I hurried back to my apartment, closed my door, locked it, and pushed my couch in front of it to secure it. After that, I went to bed and lay awake all night with the small baseball bat at my side.

Chapter 23

My cellphone rang in my left pants pocket. Rather than put the basket down that I was carrying in my left hand, I fumbled for it with my right, reaching across my body and trying to get into the pocket back handed. I didn't want to put the basket down because it was raining hard and the wicker would get wet on the ground, as would the blanket inside. The blanket was there to make the cat feel more comfortable on our way home from her surgery at the vet. She was curled up inside the basket, drowsy and comfortably oblivious to the howling gusts of October wind and the rain that was making my three-block walk home miserable. She had finally been spayed. Although I had tried to put it off and wait for her to go out of season, she never did for more that what seemed a few hours before becoming a feline pole dancer again. I finally had to bite the bullet and bring her in, paying the full price, and subjecting myself to the condemning looks and tongue clicking of the clinic staff. But it was over now, and I was on my way home with the cat, leaving their sanctimonious disapproval behind.

It never occurred to me to just pass the basket from hand to hand and then reach into the left pocket with the left hand. I managed to hook the phone out of my pocket to answer it. It was Bid.

"What the heck is all that noise?" she asked.

"Take your pick," I said, wondering why she was calling me in the middle of the day. "I'm walking on Bathurst. It might be the streetcars, wind, construction, rain, or it could be the traffic on the wet street."

"That's the one," she said. "Why are you walking in the rain?"

"I'm picking up the cat from the vet," I said. "She has been spayed and is going home to convalesce. It's just a short walk to my place, about two more blocks."

"Perfect," she clipped over the phone. "I'll see you in a few minutes. I'm standing in front of your place." The phone went dead.

She was indeed in front of my place, hunched under the shelter of the porch overhang, wearing a yellow raincoat with a matching sou'wester. Her oversized bag dangled heavily from her left hand. She was wiping the lens of her glasses with her index finger like a windshield wiper just as I rounded the corner. The rain had picked up and I was walking as quickly as I could without bouncing the recovering cat too violently. She had suffered enough, I figured.

"You look a bit like a drowned cat, yourself," Bid said laughing at me. My hair was drenched and my clothes were, too.

We were upstairs in no time and the cat was carefully lifted out of the basket and placed on the cushion I had bought her for the occasion. I towelled my hair while Bid rifled through her bag. "So, what brings you here?"

"It's about time, don't you think?" She pulled out her yellow tube of wall plaster. "We need to fix these holes that we made in your wall. It's been over a month."

"You already filled the holes with plaster," I said, "on the night we made the holes."

"You have to do it twice," she said. "You see how the plaster has contracted when it dried, making little dimples?" I couldn't see it. With a few well-placed swipes of her trowel, she had filled them to her satisfaction.

"Perfect," she said, admiring her work. "Now, when we get back here after the show tonight, they'll be dry, so I'll sand them and prime them then." She swung around to look me in the eye. "Then, you'll make me dinner, and after that I'll paint them." She turned her attention back to her bag and began pulling the sandpaper, brushes, and two tiny paint cans out of her bag, which she lined up on the coffee table. Then she headed to the kitchen sink to wash the trowel.

"Dinner?" she had taken me by surprise.

"Of course. And it better be good. I'll be working up an appetite, doing all this manual labour for you." She blinked twice at me and pushed up her glasses. Then she looked at her watch. "I have to go. See you at the theatre. Don't be late." She spun herself into her raincoat, popped her yellow hat on, and she was gone. I stood there looking at the inside of my front door. If she hadn't left the paint supplies and the wet plaster in the wall, I would have sworn I had dreamed it. All I could think was what could Bid possibly want for supper?

Once I assembled a menu, I felt good about putting supper together for Bid. After the initial shock of knowing that I had to cook her dinner, it took only a little time to organize what I wanted to prepare. Stage managers exist in a grey zone between crew and actors. Although they are members of Actors' Equity Association, to an outsider they much more resemble the technical crew. To the crew though, they fall outside the technical realm. So they occupy a kind of solitude that Bid seemed to shed suddenly. Bid had always been good to me. She constantly let me know what was happening at the theatre, and where I had to be. She nursed my injuries when we encountered the Bodinov thugs. When I had thanked her for that, she tossed it off saying, "It was nothing. I just don't want to lose an actor. Do you know how long it would take me to rehearse someone new? Sheesh!"

I had enormous respect for her and realized that she was a great friend, although, I had never really thought about it before. I just took her for granted, like you do with friends.

I headed out in the rain once more to do a bit of shopping for our dinner. I had to decide whether to make something ahead of time and warm it up, or to prepare something quickly when we came in later tonight. I settled on both. I would prepare everything in advance and bring it all together while she sanded and primed the wall. Bid was meticulous, so I decided to try and match her work ethic with something worthy. Just throwing together a frozen entrée or a premixed meal wouldn't do.

I returned with my groceries, soaked to the skin again, but ready to start everything from scratch. We would have a Caesar salad, potato-crusted halibut with carrots and broccoli, and for dessert, warm sabayon over strawberries. The more I worked on the meal, the more I enjoyed the prospect of sharing it with Bid. I created the base for the salad dressing in advance. I crushed the garlic, capers, and anchovies with a fork, and then drizzled the olive oil into the egg yolk as I mixed it with the back of a spoon until it was thick enough to stick to the bowl. I put the dressing in the fridge for later, when I would add the final ingredients. I decided to serve the salad dressing over whole leaves so I wouldn't have to cut them and risk browning edges when we returned, and I would grate the Parmesan cheese later so it wouldn't lose any of the flavour.

I washed the halibut and dusted it with flour, salt, and pepper, and I grated the potatoes into fine shreds. I had to squeeze the shreds to remove the excess water and then dip the fish in an egg wash and coat with the potato before returning the fillets to the fridge. The vegetables were in the steamer; the crispy croutons were cooling out of the oven, and the fresh strawberries were washed, hulled, and sliced.

I was in and out of the shower in minutes and was dashing for the door when I remembered to set the eggs out of the fridge for the sabayon. I was lucky to flag down a cab in front of my building, and I made it to the theatre in plenty of time.

After the show, while I was cleaning up my dressing room, Nigel popped in from the green room.

"Could you manage a few jars?" he asked, meaning a few beers at the local bar.

"Not tonight," I said. "I'm off home tonight. Maybe tomorrow."

"Yeah, you're looking a bit tired," he said. "Tomorrow it is then," and he disappeared.

I took my time meandering, waiting for Bid, and feeling a bit self-conscious staying after everyone had gone but the crew. I found Bid helping Tamara set the props on the prop table for the next day's show.

"You go on ahead," she said. "I still have a few things to do. I won't be long though."

Chapter 24

It was 11:45 when my buzzer jolted me enough that I dropped the spoon into the salad dressing as I was adding the vinegar. I ran over to the button to buzz her in with my elbow while wiping dressing from my hands with paper towel. I left the door ajar for her and went back to the kitchen. I heard the door close and saw her peek around the corner first before venturing into the kitchen, carrying a paper bag that obviously contained two bottles. Without a word, she dropped the bag on the counter and headed over to the small paint cans she had left earlier. She gave them a quick shake before popping one open and then dipped a small brush into the thin-looking white primer and swished it on.

"I wasn't sure what we were having so I brought red and white," she finally said over her shoulder. She closed the little paint can and went to the sink to wash out the brush.

"I'll let you choose which wine," I said. "We're having fish. I hope that's all right."

"Perfect," she said, as she dragged a bar stool over to the counter where I was tossing the salad. She propped herself up and started to remove the cork from the bottle of white. "I like the apron," she said.

"Some friends brought it back from Paris for me," I said. "I'm working with oil tonight and oil is impossible to get out of clothes. I'm clumsy, so I wear it."

"You know, that's one of the things I like about you: you're not afraid to be honest." She craned her neck. "You're making Caesar salad from scratch? This is impressive. Where did you learn that?"

"I've spent a lot of time as a waiter between acting jobs. Some of the places I've worked were nice and I learned a few things," I said. "What about you? You said you were in the Forces?"

"Five years," she said, pouring the wine. Then quietly she said, "There's no life like it . . . I made the mandatory five-year commitment, and the last three years I was a medic. I didn't really know what I wanted to do, so I chose that. I think even then I knew I wouldn't make a career of the army, so I chose something that would have transferable skills once I got out."

"What made you go into the army in the first place?"

"I don't really know," she said, passing me a wineglass. "Cheers," she said quietly, with her glass raised. Our glasses rang together. "I was always a bit of a loner at school; I was unlike my classmates. I had friends, but I thought they were all a bit strange, you know." She took a small sip of wine. Her face had changed over the last few minutes. Her usual confidence and strength were ebbing, and she got a faraway quality in her eyes as she talked about her past, and then caught herself, throwing out a glib comment to bring her strong persona back. "It turns out, I was the odd one.

"I started school at five so I finished high school early, at seventeen," she continued. "My friends were all a year older than me; that could have accounted for some of our differences, but I still felt we weren't on the same page. They all had grand plans for school and their future, and I not only hadn't chosen a path, I couldn't even see the choices. I don't know why I did it, but I enlisted. Maybe I was looking for a place to fit in, or maybe I was looking for an escape. My mother wanted to kill me. In the Forces, I met a lot of other people that felt the same as me: a little removed from the crowd.

"It was a good life, for a while, lots of rules, lots of opportunity, but after five years I had had enough." She took another sip. "Then I went back to school: theatre school. That's where the light went on. I really fit in there."

"I'm glad you did," I said as I put the salad onto two plates. "Go to theatre school, I mean."

She picked a small leaf off the plate as I went by her on my way to the table. "Whoa! Great dressing. I'll want the recipe."

"It's a secret," I said.

"Oh," she looked disappointed.

"I'm pulling your leg," I said apologetically as I could muster. I could see she had let her guard down and I saw vulnerability in Bid that was previously hidden to me. So I quickly added, "The secret is that no matter what you put into the dressing, you have to sprinkle lemon juice on the lettuce before you dress it."

"That's the secret?"

"I wouldn't tell just anybody." I meant that. "I'll write out the rest of the recipe for you, though."

She devoured the salad and kept pouring us wine. I got up to start the next course and she followed me with the plates to the sink. She reached for the faucet to start washing them but I touched her hand to stop her. "You can keep me company while I cook, but no washing. You are my guest."

"Okay," she shrugged and smiled. Clearly, she was enjoying this. Then she sat at the counter on the bar stool while I donned the apron to brown the fish.

Sharing a meal with someone is a great way to peek at their inner self and gives you an excuse to expose yourself in a way that you might not otherwise do. What people eat reveals only some things about them. To really get to know someone, watch how they get the food to their mouths and how they manage the food on their plates. Before beginning, Bid surveyed the plate before her. She then cut a small piece of the halibut and I noticed she furtively examined it as she brought it to her mouth. Her first bite broadened into a smile.

"Delicious. I like the crunchy potato coating," she said, then abruptly added, "Nigel told me you were once married." She popped a carrot into her mouth and waited for a comment from me.

"I was," I said. "And I made a mess of it." I tried to stop myself from going further, by taking a bite of food, but Bid waited. After a pause I surprised myself by telling her everything. "I was a fool to let it fail. Whether it was a mistake to begin with, or not, I let my circumstances direct my path. I should have created my own circumstances. My marriage didn't so much fail, but came to a stop. I am still upset with myself for allowing that to happen. Not only did the marriage fail, but *I* failed to live up to the promises I made to my ex-wife. That was most disappointing." I stopped as if something had hit me. "Sorry, I hadn't ever thought about my life that way before."

"I am also guilty of similar weaknesses," she said. "They are probably characteristic of youth." She raised her glass and said, "Let's toast our youth and welcome our adulthood by creating our own circumstances." I watched her as she put her glass to her lips. She took the smallest sip, just barely wetting her lips. Blood rushed to my face when I realized she was watching me watch her.

I was truly delighted that Bid enjoyed the meal I had prepared. She was a wonderful dinner guest, accepting seconds and commenting on the food in detail. She sampled each component of her plate separately, and then ate them together in every combination. That was the way she lived her life, I thought. She was able to see each element and then experience the whole in panorama. Talking about our food likes and preferences led us to speak about everything. We talked and spent the night telling each other not only what we thought and liked, but why we thought the way we did. We found that we both shared a feeling of, not isolation, but separateness from the rest of the world.

"I'm not sure if it is a feature of being an actor or my nature," I said, "that I find myself watching the world from the outside, evaluating the activity and the choices made by others. I rationalize by telling myself that it is an attempt at perpetual character research for my work, of course."

"I understand," she said. "It's like being a lifeguard at a pool. To anyone looking on the pool from the outside, the lifeguard is a part of the scenery, but the lifeguard feels separate from the people playing in the water. Always watchful, always vigilant, and afraid to become a part of the scene in case they lose control." Yes, she understood exactly.

We ultimately shifted to Kyle's rescue and how we were both angry at first that he was not only ungrateful but seemingly oblivious to the danger he was in, and then how he surprised us by helping me when I was in danger. I let Bid know about the visit from Frank the cop, and how I directed him to the storage place where Sal had hidden his stash of drugs.

"That was before the mess with the gunman at the storage locker," I said. "The police had probably removed the drugs before we got there."

"Have you heard from the cop since then?" she asked.

"Not a word," I said.

"I read in the paper this morning about Robert Eaton, Kyle's father," she changed the subject. "It looks like he is the front-runner in the Conservative Party leadership race."

"Is that what the sequestered meeting was all about, when he had to fly to Ottawa?"

"That's what I think," said Bid as I put dessert in front of her. "That's probably why they wanted to keep the police as far away from Kyle as possible."

When she put the first spoonful of sabayon and strawberries into her mouth, she stood and applauded. "I have never had anything like this before."

She opened the second bottle of wine as we started the dishes. We finished the last few sips sitting side by side on the couch with our feet on the coffee table, just as the sun began to rise. The breaking dawn revealed that the rain had stopped.

"This is nice," she said stretching and looking at her watch, "but I have to go. We have a Sunday night show to do tonight and I want to get some sleep."

I wanted to protest, to stop her from feeling that she had to leave. The night had slipped past us and I just wanted to continue talking. I thought if she left, this would all disappear. She was right though. We had a show tonight.

She slipped her rain hat into the sleeve of her raincoat, rolled up the rain coat, and stuffed it into her bag.

"We never did paint the wall," I said, looking at the patchy primed area on the wall.

"Hmm, I guess I'll have to come back another time to do that." She slung her bag up onto her shoulder. "You'll want to have that done soon, too. . . . Probably tonight. Shall I cook this time?" She didn't wait for a response before declaring, "Get some wine." She put down her bag and walked over to me. She pushed her glasses higher up onto her nose and reached up to kiss my cheek. There was no way she could have reached it without help, so I leaned in. It was the most delicate kiss, her lips barely touching me. I suddenly felt light-headed, and it had nothing to do with the wine. Then she took off her glasses, wrapped her arms around my neck, and kissed my mouth.

"Can I come back tonight and cook?" She asked as if I would possibly have said no.

"I can't wait," I said. "Shall I get red or white?"

"Yes," she said with a very large smile. She looked as happy as I felt.

I was leaning in to kiss her, when urgent knocking erupted at my door. It shook me a bit. Who could be knocking on doors at six thirty on a Sunday morning?

I opened the door to find Dennis looking apologetic and Frank the cop looking serious.

"Good morning," said Frank. "Can we come in?" He was already by me.

"Dennis, right?" said Bid holding her hand out to shake his. "We met a few weeks ago. There were a few of us here though; you may not remember me."

"Of course I remember you," said Dennis, taking her hand. "You were the one in charge that night."

"That's her," I said. "Dennis, Frank, this is Elizabeth Stackhouse."

"Bid," she corrected me.

"Sorry about knocking on your door at this hour, but we heard you were awake," said Dennis.

"You can hear sounds from my apartment through the walls?"

"No, I heard the water running in the sink," said Dennis. "Your kitchen sink and mine share the same wall. I could also hear you

226

putting away dishes in the cupboards above the sink. Say, isn't this pretty early for you?"

"Late," I said. "We were cleaning up the dinner dishes. What's going on?"

"Can we talk?" said Frank, indicating Bid. "Were you involved in the Bodinov affair?"

"Of course," said Dennis. "She was in charge." Bid put her bag down.

"Has something gone wrong with Bodinov?" I asked, expecting the worst. "Are we in trouble?"

"Not really," said Frank, tentatively. "But, you had better sit down."

"I'm fine," I said not believing it. "Just get it over with. Wait — what do you mean *not really*?"

"I need your help again," said Frank. "The last time, you helped us without knowing it. This time we're coming to you."

"What do you mean, last time, this time," I said. "There is no *this time*. I put my friends at risk the last time and that's just what it was . . . the last time . . . the only time."

Frank said nothing, just hung his head as if he were formulating what he wanted to say next.

"Look, I'm not an investigator or a detective," I almost whined. "I'm an actor. I play at make-believe for a living. That's all we were doing to help out a friend."

"Let me explain," said Frank. "What you did the last time wasn't strictly legal, and I took a bit of heat for it. Don't get me wrong. I didn't keep you out of it because I'm a nice guy. I did it because we needed to arrest that guy Sal and you made it easy for us, and convenient. If I had admitted to knowing how you did it, and why, there would have been a whole new angle that would likely have led

227

to Bodinov's release, and would have put you and a few others in grave danger. That kid, his parents, and even Dennis would have been in the soup. Bodinov's attorney would probably have suggested that the police orchestrated the whole thing, and it would have been thrown out of court.

"You can bet the press would have run with it, too. Everybody would have been named, including you, and that would have been disastrous. So, I just let it be, hoping it would all fade away. But there were some unanswered questions and loose ends that people kept asking about. I couldn't answer the questions, so naturally I just shrugged my shoulders and people began to assume another agency was responsible for the setup. I kept on shrugging my shoulders until the other agencies came calling, wondering why I was pointing the finger at them. I wasn't of course. Everybody just made assumptions."

"What other agencies?" I asked.

"The feds," he said.

"The RCMP? Oh, God!" I was starting to panic.

"And CSIS," Frank added.

"Okay, this is starting to look very serious," said Bid. "Do they know we're involved?"

"Yes."

"Then, why aren't they here now?" she asked, while I simply cradled my head in my hands.

"They wanted to be," he said, shifting his weight. "I told them I would make contact first, and then we would all meet. I was going to try to see you sometime later today, but when I heard you were up, I thought I would talk to you sooner than later."

"I think we have to hear him out," Bid said, looking at me, which took me by surprise. She gave me a look that compelled me to agree to at least hear the story.

228

Frank turned to Dennis. "For your protection, I am going to ask you to leave now." Dennis's face sank, but he knew Frank was right.

"I'll see you later," was how he left us and closed the door behind him.

"There is a group we have been watching for some time," Frank quietly said to us, after he heard my door click shut. "We think they are planning some kind of mischief. But, we need to know exactly what they are planning and when. There's no real danger. We just need some eyes and ears inside their group."

"Mischief?" asked Bid. "What kind of mischief?"

"We've intercepted some communications from them," he said carefully. "We think they are planning to blow something up and we have a pretty good idea what the target is. We just want to know if it's a serious threat, or if they're a bunch of crackpots."

"What kind of communications?" asked Bid. "And what are they planning to blow up?"

"First I have to know, are you in? If you're not, the feds won't let the Bodinov thing rest. I'm not threatening you. I'm just letting you know what they told me."

Bid looked at me.

"We don't really have a choice do we," I said quietly, and she shook her head. We were stuck. "Before I can agree to anything, I have a few conditions first." Frank's gaze shot over to me with a start. "We have four weeks left in the run of our show, and we have a dinner engagement tonight. We cannot miss either of those." Bid tried not to smile.

"Fine," said Frank.

"What do you think?" I asked Bid, taking her hand. She pumped my hand twice. I sighed. "Okay, we're in."

Acknowledgements

My sincere thanks to Ian Shaw of Deux Voiliers Publishing for taking a chance on a first-time novelist. Thanks to editor Bill Horne for his advice and encouragement, and to Tom Thompson for his insight on police procedures.

To my brilliant editor Paula Sarson, whose support knows no bounds, and for her deft and tactful use of the red pen, I offer my deepest gratitude. I thank Ania Szneps for her meticulous proofreading and e-book formatting. And finally, to every actor, stage manager and stage tech I have ever worked with: thank you.

About Gerry Fostaty

Gerry Fostaty is the author of *As You Were: The Tragedy at Valcartier*. *Stage Business* is his first novel. He was an actor working on stage and in film and television for more than twenty years.

About Deux Voiliers Publishing

Organized as a writers-plus collective, Deux Voiliers Publishing is a new generation publisher. We focus on high quality works of fiction by emerging Canadian writers. The art of creating new works of fiction is our driving force.

We are proud to have published *Stage Business* by Gerry Fostaty.

Other Works of Fiction published by Deux Voiliers Publishing

Soldier, Lily, Peace and Pearls by Con Cú (Literary Fiction 2012)

Kirk's Landing by Mike Young (Crime/Adventure 2014)

Sumer Lovin' by Nicole Chardenet (Humour/Fantasy 2013)

Last of the Ninth by Stephen Lorne Bennett (Historical Fiction 2012)

Marching to Byzantium by Brendan Ray (Historical Fiction 2012)

Tales of Other Worlds by Chris Turner (Fantasy/Science Fiction 2012)

Romulus by Fernand Hibbert and translated by Matthew Robertshaw (Historical Fiction/English Translation 2014)

Bidong by Paul Duong (Literary Fiction 2012)

Zaidie and Ferdele by Carol Katz (Illustrated Children's Fiction 2012)

Palawan Story by Caroline Vu (Literary Fiction 2014)

Cycling to Asylum by Su J. Sokol (Speculative Fiction 2014)

Please visit our website for ordering information
www.deuxvoilierspublishing.com

35802745R00146

Made in the USA
Charleston, SC
18 November 2014